The Scented Flowers of Sinjin-Ka

The Scented Flowers of Sinjin-Ka

Martin Hart

ASAT Press
Topsfield, Massachusetts

Published by ASAT Press.

Created with Verbii.com.

For press and media related inquiries, contact: Martin Hart, asat@asat.org

Paperback / Softcover ISBN: 9780989551809

Ebook ISBN: 9780989551816

Digitised book: 9780989551823

Library of Congress Control Number: 2013910981

Copies are available at special rates for bulk orders. Contact the sales team at ASAT Press, asat@asat.org

Dedication

For all my seen and unseen friends;
forever in Love and Light

Table of Contents

Prologue

High in the Celestial Mountains, in a remote cave,
sat the Great and Holy Sinjin-Ka
deep in meditation.

He sat this way for a hundred years,
bathing in the waters of Eternal Bliss,
at peace in the nurturing womb of the Divine.

One night, during the magic of the twilight time,
Sinjin-Ka opened his eyes.

When the people heard of this,
they gathered at his feet.

And each night, for ninety-one nights,
during the magic of the twilight time,
Sinjin-Ka told all who gathered
a story.

Listen, my beloved, and listen well,
to the stories that he,
the Great and Holy Sinjin-Ka,
told during the magic of the twilight time.

1

The Fool and the Apple

In a sacred banyan grove,
beneath an ancient Grandmother Tree,
a Master sat meditating on the nature of desire.

After some time,
he opened his eyes and spoke.

"I hunger for an apple. How shall I fulfill
this desire?"

His disciples thought deeply on the matter.

The Farmer spoke first.

"O' beloved Master,
I'll plant for you an apple seed.
In a few years, when the seed becomes
a ripened tree,
I'll pick for you the finest of its fruit."

ॐ

"What silliness!"
laughed the General.
"Would you make our Master wait
years to satisfy his craving?

I have a better way.

O' beloved Master,
the Kingdom of Jahar is famous for its apples.
With my mighty army, I'll win
for you an apple,
and thus you'll have what you desire,
and it will only take a month."

ॐ

"Only one apple?"
laughed the Merchant,

I have a better way.

O' beloved Master,
I'll journey alone to the markets of Jahar
and buy for you a bushel of their finest
tasty fruits.
Then, when you desire, you'll have one at
your reach."

ॐ

"This is craziness!"
shouted the Chief Minister,

"I have a better way.

O' beloved Master,
the splendid groves of Kaladar are
only a day away.
I'll negotiate with the farmers there
to fulfill your heart's desire.
You shall have your precious apple in a day;
not years or many months."

⚜

"I cannot believe my ears!"
chuckled the Farmer's Wife.

"I have a better way.

O' beloved Master,
down the road is the village market.
I'll buy a bushel of their sweetest fruit.
Your desire shall be fulfilled in less
than an hour;
not days, or months, or years."

⚜

"How absurd!"
snickered the King.

"I have a better way.

O' beloved Master,
I'll tax my loyal subjects a quarter

of their savings, and in this way
satisfy a lifetime of your cravings."

෨෮

"Children, children!"
whimpered the saintly Priest,
"Children, where's your faith?

It's God on high, and God above,
who has the better way.

O' beloved Master,
let us pray to Him Supreme,
that he in all his infinite mercy
shall shower down the most heavenly fruits
you'll ever want or need."

He looked to the Master for approval.

෨෮

But the Master did not notice,
nor did he hear the others,
but looked instead to a nearby banyan tree.

There he saw lying amid the
tree's many roots,
a fool eating a juicy apple.

To his amazement,
he noticed that each time the fool
finished an apple
he would reach out his hand

and from the branches of the
fruitless banyan tree
an apple fell into it.

"Fool!" cried the Master,
"How do you get apples from a barren
banyan tree?
I desire to know your secret. I wish to
learn your magic."

While gazing lovingly at his apple,
the fool wistfully replied,

"Life's an illusion, dear friend.
You can have as much of an illusion
as you wish.

You only need to ask,
but, most of all, be willing to receive."

He laughed as another ripe red apple
fell into his awaiting hand.

The Master smiled, closed his eyes,
and returned to his meditation, satisfied.

Meanwhile,
his disciples continued arguing
among themselves
the best ways to fulfill a desire.

The fool dined on yet another fruit
he so willingly received.

2

Not Enough Enough

"Go build for me a marble palace,"
said the Master to a disciple,
and handed him a hammer and a chisel.

"But, Master, this is not enough,"
said the disciple,
"I will need much more."

So, the Master gave the disciple more.

A year went by, and the Master
asked the disciple,
"How comes my marble palace?"

"O' Master, I do not have enough,"
replied the disciple.
"I will need much more."

So, the Master gave the disciple more.

Another year went by, and again
the Master asked,
"How comes my marble palace?"

"O' Master, I'm not enough,"
replied the disciple.
"I'm much in need of learning."

So, the Master arranged for a master builder
to teach the disciple all he needed to know.

☙❧

Another year went by, and again
the Master asked,
"How comes my marble palace?"

"O' Master, still there's not enough,"
whined the disciple.
"And, there's yet more for me to learn!"

The Master then turned to a blind disciple
and said,

"Build for me a marble palace,"
and gave him a tiny feather.

☙❧

The blind disciple returned in three months.

With only three months, and a tiny feather,
he built for his Master
a most magnificent marble palace.

Three months, and a tiny feather,
were far more than he needed.

3

Where the Animals Went to Die

When the Master finished his lesson on
'The Beauty of the Human Heart,'
he listened patiently as one by one,
his followers asked their questions
and to their satisfaction,
he answered all with insight and compassion.

After a while,
an old woman stood up and spoke.

"O' wise Teacher," she said,
"my heart is very heavy.

Why do wild things come to me,
so old and sick, are they?
I care for them for a little while,
then in my arms, they die."

"O' loving mother, can you not see?"
replied the Master.
"They come to you to die.

You're their earthly mother
on their way to Mother Divine,
and your heart is the loving harbor they seek
upon their journey home.

They come to stay a little while
to be nurtured by your love,
then, with gratitude,
pass from your embracing arms
into Her Embracing Love."

"But my heart pains so at their loss,"
wept the old woman.

"And so, it must, dear one; and so, it must,"
was the Master's tender reply.

"Grief is how we heal.
It makes our love grow stronger.

Forget this not, dear mother.
Your love becomes Her Embracing Love
when you give your heart, and from your heart,
love's freedom."

The old woman cried deeply
and thanked her wise and beloved teacher.

ೞೞ

Throughout the remaining years of her life
she gave loving shelter
to the many creatures who came to her to die.

ౠౠ

When the time came for her to pass,
she laid peacefully upon her bed
and gently closed her eyes,
while hundreds of wild creatures
gathered around her humble home
to see her on her way to
Her Embracing Love.

4

The Disciple and the Idiot

A Master went in search of his truant disciple.

When he came to the edge of a ripple-less sea,
he found the disciple kneeling at the feet
of an idiot.
The idiot, giggling with glee,
was happily engaged in throwing rocks
into the ripple-less sea.

"O' wayward disciple!" scolded the Master,
"Why are you neglecting your studies
and daily meditations?
Why are you kneeling here at the feet
of this foolish man?"

"O' great Master, I'm learning much
from my friend," replied the disciple.
"You have awakened my mind
by your teachings,
my friend has awakened my heart."

The Master became very angry.

"Oh, impudent boy, what is there to learn here?
This idiot knows nothing of the Sacred Texts,
or the ways of the enlightened ones.

He wears one shoe, and his pants
are on backward,
and he smiles with a silly grin.
What is there he could possibly teach you?"

"He teaches me how to laugh and play,"
answered the disciple,
"And he teaches me to dance with abandon,
and to see the world as new.

Together we stare in rapped attention
at the wonders of an anthill,
and, with solemn purpose,
gather the magic stones
that lie upon the sand.

He teaches me to see the simple things,
and to marvel at their complexity.
But most of all, he teaches me how to love,
and how to wonder,
and how to know what's real.

And he teaches me how the Wise Fool lives;
the most blessed of the enlightened."

ಬಾಲ

The Master became silent.

He knew his disciple found in this foolish man
what he for a lifetime sought.
And thought how empty his life had been
for not having such a teacher.

The Master knelt beside the disciple,
and at the feet of the idiot,
became his disciple, too.

The idiot, giggling with glee,
happily threw another rock
into the ripple-less sea.

5

A Gift from a Squished Squirrel

A woman was driving her cart to market.

Suddenly, a squirrel scurried out in front
of her
and got squished beneath her wheel;
a mangled mess of fur.

The woman wailed loudly,

"Oh, no! Oh, no! What have I done!
I've taken the life of this poor creature!
What a wretched soul am I!"

She spent the remainder of the day
in weepy self-pity,
and wallowing in her own self-loathing.

That night, while she slept,
the squirrel appeared to her in a dream;
radiant and un-squished.

"Stop your ballyhooing!" scolded the squirrel.
"You did not kill me!

I chose this fate, or better said,
the unconscious part of me.

I was crossing over anyway, and you so
kindly helped.
Take my death as a gift, dear lady,
a gift from me to you.

I ask that you now accept it!

The shame you feel is not from to me,
but lurks in a place inside you.
It's the false belief you're wrong or bad,
or broken, or flawed,
or defective in some strange way.

None of this is true.

My death brought up this shame in you
that you may know and feel it.
And if you will be free of this,
then choose, dear one, to heal it.

So, stop your senseless blame and guilt
and feel this shame within you;

this shame from pains of many wounds
you felt so long ago.

Then, if you're willing, forgive yourself
and simply let them go."

శంఖ

The next morning the woman woke
and chose to feel her shame.

She screamed and wept,
felt anger and hurt,
from wounds she locked in a hidden place
so very deep inside her.

She cried, and wept, and felt her pain
till she could feel the pain no more.

Then she forgave herself,
and let it go,
and thanked the squirrel who saved her.

శంఖ

Later that day,
she climbed on her cart
and happily drove to market
without incident.

6

The Doll Maker's Helper

There lived a famous maker of dolls
whose wondrous creations gave joy to every child.

In villages far and wide,
laughter and the gleeful sounds of play
resounded from every home,
so marvelous were the beautiful dolls he made.

One day,
the doll maker noticed that his old helper
was most unhappy.
He did not smile. He did not laugh.
He just sat alone in silence.

"What troubles you, old friend?"
asked the doll maker.
"It pains me to see you so unhappy."

"Master, you're such a gifted soul,"
replied the old man.

"Your creations bring joy and happiness,
and you're beloved throughout the land.
What you craft lifts the hearts of all.

I, on the other hand, am an old man
whose days are nearly over.
I'm not blessed with special gifts
like you;
no talent do I possess.

Painting eyes on your beautiful dolls
is all I know how to do.
I've accomplished nothing in life.

And not one soul shall remember me,
or recognize the work I've done."

A tear trickled down the old man's cheek.

"Old friend, listen closely to what I say,"
said the doll maker, tenderly.

"Who you are, and what you do,
are more precious than you know.

Look at these faceless dolls, my friend.
They're lifeless without the eyes you give them.

When children gaze at their beloved dolls,
and behold the painted eyes looking back,
they laugh, and they are happy.

Yes, they do not know your name,
but does that truly matter?

When you reflect upon your life, my friend,
value the joy you gave to others,
and the happiness you give to me."

The old man thought for a while
on the doll maker's words,
then returned to his work.

He painted two eyes on a blank wooden face,
stared at it for a while, like an artist to his canvass,
then smiled.

7

The Witch of the Darkened Wood

"Never enter the Darkened Wood!"
the people of the village warned her.

"An old witch lives within; a vile and evil hag.
And with her spells, she'll drive you mad,
and with her charms, she'll bind you.
You'll never be seen again, my dear,
for she shall surely find you.

Some have heard her laugh,
some have heard her sing,
and in the fullness of the silver moon,
some have seen her dance
wild and naked in the moon's soft light."

"Never enter the Darkened Wood!"
the people of the village warned her.

"An old witch lives within; a vile and evil hag."

But her heart was heavy, and much in pain,
and so in need of help was she,
she decided against all wit and reason
to enter the Darkened Wood.

She heard the stories of ancient magic;
of wonderous, mighty workings.

And she heard of the few who ventured forth,
and of the healing each one found there
from some strange enchanted magic.

So, into the Darkened Wood she went
among the ancient trees,
and walked its rivers, and climbed its hills,
and journeyed among its wild things.

She felt a fear not felt before from a deep
and primal source,
but despite her fear, and despite her dread,
the girl kept venturing forth.

ഇൗ

In time, she came to a clearing
in the heart of the Darkened Wood,
and beheld a most beautiful cottage
covered in vines of flowers.

Beside the cottage, a small garden
lush with healing herbs,
and from the heart of this little garden
she heard a woman singing.

An ancient woman with back bent low from age
walked lightly from the garden
as if upon the air.

She smiled lovingly at the frightened girl
and ever so brightly said,

"Welcome, my child. I've been expecting you!
Come to my house and sit awhile.
There's delicious tea, and tasty biscuits,
waiting for you there."

The old woman entered her flowered cottage,
followed reluctantly by the girl.

"Sit here, my child." The old crone said,
pointing to a table.
The girl sat down at the end of it,
the old woman at the other.

The old woman placed a cup of tea
and a plate of biscuits
before the frightened girl.

"Here, my child, have some tea
and have a tasty biscuit,
and tell old granny what troubles thee,
and speak it from your heart."

The girl sipped the tea, and ate a biscuit,
then began to tell her story.

The more she sipped, and the more she ate,
the more at ease she felt.

The old crone, speaking not a word,
gave full attention to all the young girl said.

ಬಌ

The girl talked and wept, and wept and talked
for an hour, or two, or more,
and, in time, felt her burden lifting.

And the old crone, speaking not a word,
listened patiently to all she said.

But, from time to time,
when the girl could no longer speak,
so deep in pain was she,
the old woman would gently say to her,

"Here, my child, have more tea
and have another biscuit,
and tell old granny what troubles thee,
and speak it from your heart."

ಬಌ

When the girl unburdened her heavy pain,
and nothing more remained to be said,
and no more tears were wept,
she felt a lightness and an inner peace
and a glowing warmth inside her.

She knew, in her heart, a healing had occurred
and a miracle was performed.

She bid a sad farewell to the kind old woman,
and journeyed home again;
happy, and light, and free.

Such is the healing magic of Ancient Ones.

It's a magic not of words, or spells, or charms,
or wondrous herbs.
It is, instead, a more powerful magic;
the magic of their hearts.

"Here, my child, have some tea
and have a tasty biscuit,
and tell old granny what troubles thee,
and speak it from your heart."

8

Standing Before the Judge

There was much she wanted from her life,
and much she wanted to give it,
but when she asked her judge within
for permission to have these things,
his verdict would be, "No!"

And she never lived the life
she always wished to live.

She wanted a loving partner and a loving family,
and wanted to spend the remainder of her life
in the expanding of her heart.

But when she asked her judge within
for permission to have these things,
his verdict would be, "No!"

And she never found the love
she was always looking for.

ಜಾ౬ಾ

She wanted success and accomplishment,
and to do great and wonderful things.

But when she asked her judge within
for permission to have it so,
his verdict would be, "No!"

And she never achieved fulfillment
in anything she did.

ಜಾ౬ಾ

She wanted to play, and race, and dance,
and to live her life happy, wild, and free.

But when she asked her judge within
for permission to have these things,
his verdict would be, "No!"

And her life became a prison
of failed hopes and dreams.

ಜಾ౬ಾ

Follow not the path of this condemned
and imprisoned woman.

Forgive yourself for what you did,
or mistakenly thought you did.

And, most of all, forgive yourself
for holding on to the lies you hold;
those lies you tell yourself.

"I'm not loved, not good enough,
not worthy, not of value."

Tell yourself these lies no more.

ॐ

And when you lie to yourself no more,
then stand before your judge within.
His verdict will be different now.

Stand tall and free before your judge
with confidence and with courage!

Stand tall and free before your judge
and be the author of your life!

Stand tall and free before your judge
forgiven and forgiving!

Stand tall and free before your judge
and listen, now, as he gives his verdict.

"Yes!"

ॐ

Be free! Be free, beloved!

Now, go wildly into your life
and start the living of it.

9

The Love of Winning

Two runners competed, but only one would win.
So, they gave the race their best
without malice, harm, or cheating.

Each dug deep within herself and found that
"something more."

But, in the end, there would be only one.

Each runner knew the other helped
in bringing out her best,
and that she, in truth, needed the other.

And there was great love in that.

Two princes vied for the throne,
but only one would win.
So, they gave the people the best
of themselves
without hatred or division.

Each dug deep within himself and found that
"something more."

But, in the end, there would be only one.

Each prince knew the other helped
in bringing out his best,
and that he, in truth, needed the other.

And there was great love in that.

ॐ

Two merchants competed for a customer,
but only one would win.
So, they offered the person the best they had
without bitterness or misleading.

Each dug deep within herself and found that
"something more."

But, in the end, there would be only one.

Each merchant knew the other helped
in bringing out her best,
and that she, in truth, needed the other.

And there was great love in that.

ॐ

Two men sought a woman's heart,
but only one would win.
So, they opened their sheltered selves

and revealed themselves to her
without jealousy or deception.

Each dug deep within himself and found that
"something more."

But, in the end, there would be only one.

Each man knew the other helped
in bringing out his best,
and that he, in truth, needed the other.

And there was great love in that.

སྦྱོཪ

Those who watched such competitions
believed winning's at the finish,
but those who fought, and played the game,
found winning in the playing.

All became better for the chase,
and of their love of winning.

But, most of all, the *"better"* came
from the love of those they chased.

And, because of the great love in that,
there was never only one.

སྦྱོཪ

But that was a long time ago.

Things are much different now.

10

Gobi's Tiny Seeds

Gobi was a great and powerful magician,
though no one ever heard of him,
or of his wondrous magic.

He was only a poor farmer
content to spend his days working his field,
and tend lovingly to his sheep and chickens.

He knew not of spells or charms,
or magic incantations,
or any of the other things magicians
knew and used
in the workings of their magic.

He only worked his field,
and tended lovingly to his sheep and chickens,
and sat beneath a willow tree
to dream his dreams of hope.

Gobi was good at dreaming.
He practiced it every day.
But Gobi's dreams were not your
average dreams;
whatever Gobi dreamed, those dreams would
someday happen.

છ૭ભ

Once, when his beloved sheep fell ill
and were on the verge of dying,
Gobi sat beneath his willow tree
and dreamed a dream of hope.

The dream became tiny seeds he held
within his hand;
then in his mind, he planted them
among his precious flock.

Soon, his beloved sheep miraculously
recovered.

છ૭ભ

When Gobi heard of a savage war
in some far off distant land,
he sat beneath his willow tree
and dreamed a dream of hope.

The dream became tiny seeds he held
within his hand;
then in his mind, he planted them
in that far off distant land.

Soon, both sides started talking,
and the war miraculously ended.

෨ඬ

When a deadly plague broke out,
and scores of people died,
Gobi sat beneath his willow tree
and dreamed a dream of hope.

The dream became tiny seeds he held
within his hand;
then in his mind, he planted them
throughout the stricken land.

Soon, healers found a cure
and, miraculously, the deadly plague subsided.

෨ඬ

No one ever heard of Gobi, or of his
wondrous magic,
but that was fine with Gobi.

He was content to work his field
and tend lovingly to his sheep and chickens,
and sit beneath his willow tree
to dream his dreams of hope.

11

The Testing of Amit Don

When Amit Don was a young child,
those older and wiser would often tell him,

"Life is a series of tests, Amit Don.
They're given to you by God.
Do well, and you shall surely pass
through the Gates of Heaven."

So, heeding their wise counsel,
Amit Don went forth through life
and bravely faced its many tests.

He struggled mightily against all the odds
and overcame life's many obstacles and pains.
And when he suffered hardship and loss,
he did so with grace and style.

And through it all, he would say to himself,

"Life is a series of tests, Amit Don.
They're given to you by God.

Do well, and you shall surely pass
through the Gates of Heaven."

ॐ

When Amit Don fell in love
and felt the stinging hurt of its loss,
he knew he was being tested.

When Amit Don had dreams and hopes
and those dreams and hopes failed,
he knew he was being tested.

When Amit Don experienced happiness,
knowing, of course,
it would soon come crashing down, and it did,
he knew he was being tested.

And through it all, he would say to himself,

"Life is a series of tests, Amit Don.
They're given to you by God.
Do well, and you shall surely pass
through the Gates of Heaven."

ॐ

When Amit Don left this life and entered
the life beyond,
he beheld a long line of souls
waiting to enter Heaven.

All held in their hands a paper;
the results of their life's tests.

Amit Don, paper in hand, confidently
joined the line.

The line was so long he could not see
it's beginning.
He just waited, and waited,
and moved forward ever so slowly.

After what seemed like eons of time,
Amit Don arrived at last
at the line's beginning.

He stood before the Gates of Heaven,
but, to his great surprise,
found no guardian there;
no one to grade his paper.

Then, to his shock and horror,
he saw a sign that read,

Welcome to Heaven
Please enter
Oh, and by the way, please throw away
those silly papers
There never was a test

God

P.S.
I hope you enjoyed the gift of life
I'd given you.

Did you have fun?

12

The Man Who Walked Backward

One day, a disciple,
confused as to the direction of his life,
asked his teacher,

"Sir, in what direction should my life go?'

"Why, forward my son, forward."
the teacher replied.
"There's power in the forward;
power in your futures yet to come.

Dream your futures before you.
Let go of the stories of your past.
There's power in your becoming,
little in where you've been."

The teacher continued.
"Listen, my son, and listen well to the story
I will tell you.

There lived a man who walked backward.
He never knew where he was going
because all he saw was where he'd been.

He would always complain,
" My life is going nowhere other than
where it's been.
But if I can only fix what was,
my life can move forward once again?"

So, he placed his hopes on healing his past
and ignored his future's call.

Sadly, for him, it's not in his past,
but his future,
all his hopes are lived.

He fixed and fixed, and healed and healed,
and tried to change his past,
but nothing ever changed for him
for all that was is no longer real.

Meanwhile, his futures passed him by
like logs adrift upon a river
flowing unnoticed in the night.

So set was he on fixing, he had no time
for becoming,

and he continued walking backward
for the remainder of his life.

As he lay dying, he whispered sadly,
'Now that I am dying, and look back
upon my life,
I see my dreams as passing mists,
and a life that never changed.'

ೞೞ

The teacher then gave this instruction
to his beloved disciple.

"Walk forward, my son, and never back,
and boldly face your futures yet to be.
Walk ahead, my son, with grace and hope,
with courage and commitment.

Dream on, my son! Dream on!
The mists today are the rivers of tomorrow.

And if your past comes up to block your way,
then, and only then, take it as it comes."

13

The Saint
Who Could Not Be Harmed

There lived a holy man
whose fame spread far and wide,
for no matter what he did, or where he went,
no harm would ever befall him.

One day, his disciples found the Saint
sitting in a pit of cobras.

The serpents wrapped themselves about him
like vines around a log,
but he just sat and calmly smiled
and marveled at their beauty.

When asked why it was, they did not bite him,
he simply replied,

"Nothing in life can harm you,
unless you allow it so."

One day, while strolling along a narrow
mountain trail,
the Saint tripped and fell into the valley
a thousand feet below.

But he just got up, brushed himself off,
and strolled back up the mountain.

When asked why it was, he was barely scratched,
he simply replied,

"Nothing in life can harm you,
unless you allow it so."

One day, when returning from a pilgrimage,
he found his house ablaze.

He calmly walked inside the house,
and amid the engulfing flames,
fetched his favorite shawl.

When asked why it was the fire did not burn him,
he simply replied,

"Nothing in life can harm you,
unless you allow it so."

As the years went by, his fame grew and spread
till there was not a man, woman, or child

who did not know of
'The Saint Who Could Not Be Harmed.'

So, when he died,
and his body placed upon a funeral
bed of flowers,
it was no surprise that people far and wide
gathered to bid farewell.

၏ၵႎ

Two men approached the funeral bed
and started arguing.
Loud and angry were they.

"He is a saint!" yelled one.
"He cannot be!" shouted the other.

And on and on they argued
over how a saint who could not be harmed
could someday up and die.

The Saint opened his eyes, looked sternly
at the men, and said,

"Gentlemen, please!
Take your discussion elsewhere
and let me enjoy my nap!"

He then laid back, and closed his eyes,
and smiled a contented smile.

For nothing in life, including death,
is there to harm you unless you allow it so.

14

What Danila Learned of Love

The village came together in joyful preparation
for the wedding of Danila and her love.

Trees were hung with garlands
of brightly colored flowers,
candles placed everywhere, and flower petals
strewn upon the ground.

The men busily assembled the marriage
canopy, and talked of their work,
and of the harvest yet to come.

Children watched in eager anticipation
as their mothers prepared sweetmeats
for the wedding feast that night.

The old men sat and talked of days
long gone,
while the old women sat shaking their heads
at the old men talking:
The old men that they loved.

Young lovers strolled along the river,
as young lovers always did;
their eyes only for each other,
unaware of the happenings all about them.

And, as was the custom at all weddings,
two Ancient Ones appeared:
The Crone, to give counsel to the bride,
and the Hermit, to the man she loved.

The Crone sat with Danila
beneath the Wedding Tree
and spoke these words to her,
words she spoke a million times before.

"Listen, my child, and listen well,
that your love may grow and prosper.

Love is constant but never consistent.
Like the sea, it ebbs and flows.
It's a dance, my child, of coming together,
and a dance of moving apart.

There are times when love will make you one,
and times when its needs must part you.
You must honor both, my dear:
the oneness and the parting.

Think of the dying of cloth,
and in so doing, understand this eternal
dance of love.

To turn a cloth of white to red,
you place it in a vat of dye
and immerse it in the color.

Then take the cloth, now soaked in red,
and hang it out to dry.

The sun will fade the red,
leaving only a trace behind,
but what remains is permanent,
and will never disappear.

As you continue this ritual
of the soaking and the drying,
more and more the red remains,
and what remains will last.

It is this dance of the soaking and the drying
that turns the white to red
and keeps it so forever.

Soak in your love as one, my child,
but don't forget the drying.

By honoring those times when you must part,
your love becomes all the stronger;
this is how my precious child,
your love will grow and last."

છઉ

The words were given.
The ancient ritual now complete.

Danila thanked the Crone and went forth
to dance her dance of love,
like a million Danilas before her.

"But, wait!" you ask.
"What did the Hermit say her husband
soon to be?"

Oh, that's a story for another time.

15

How the Master
Found Enlightenment

Three disciples sat for many years
at the feet of their enlightened Master.

They memorized the Sacred Texts,
but did not understand them.

They meditated day and night,
but all they did was sleep.

They chanted the Holy Verses,
but found them much too boring.

They said to themselves,
"There must be a better way
to reach ever-elusive enlightenment."

When the Master passed beyond
into the Eternal Oneness,
the three disciples said to each other,

"Let us contemplate upon our dear Master's life,
that we may find the secret way
to ever-elusive enlightenment."

And so, they sat together for a long time,
contemplating.

ಬಂಜ

The first disciple spoke.

"Our Master always ate strawberries.
Perhaps by eating strawberries, we shall find
enlightenment."

They all agreed,
and spent many years eating nothing but
strawberries.

They taught others
The Sacred Way of Strawberry Eating
and wrote books extolling the virtues
of strawberries in gaining liberation.

But this did not help them find
ever-elusive enlightenment.

Again, they sat together for a long-time,
contemplating.

ಬಂಜ

The second disciple spoke.

"Our Master always danced naked in the
lavender fields.
Perhaps dancing naked in lavender
is the means to gain enlightenment."

They all agreed and spent many tiring years
dancing naked in lavender fields.

They taught others
*'The Sacred Way of Dancing Naked
in Lavender Fields'*
and wrote books extolling the virtues of naked
dancing in gaining liberation.

But this did not help them find
ever-elusive enlightenment.

Again, they sat together for a long-time,
contemplating.

ಬಿಂಬ

The third disciple spoke.

"Our Master always stroked his long
white beard.
Perhaps stroking long white beards
is the means to gain enlightenment."

They all agreed, concluding that enlightenment
was only available to men,
and spent many years stroking their long
white beards.

They taught others, men only of course,
'The Sacred Way of Beard-Stroking'
and wrote books extolling the virtues of
beard-stroking in gaining liberation.

But this did not help them find
ever-elusive enlightenment.

Frustrated, they gave up their pursuit
of enlightenment,
finding it much too elusive,
and went and got drunk.

16

The Man Who Said,
"Thank You."

There lived a most unusual man
who always said, "thank you."

Not just at times of good fortune,
but at times of misfortune, too.

The people of his village thought him daft,
but would not say so to his face,
for he was such a pleasant man.

Once when his purse was stolen,
he was heard to say,

"Thank you, Mother Divine,
for the money I was given,
and for the money yet to come.
May the thief enjoy his new-found riches."

Once, when he broke his leg,
and was unable to walk for weeks,
he was heard to say,

"Thank you, Mother Divine,
for slowing me down.
My life was going much too fast.

Now I have time to reflect on what
needs reflecting,
and to enjoy the fragrance of my garden."

Once, when his lovely cottage burned
to the ground,
along with all his earthly possessions,
he wept, of course,
but then was heard to say,

"Thank you, Mother Divine,
for my lovely home,
and for all my wonderful possessions.

And thank you for my new home yet to come,
and for all I shall place within it."

When his beloved wife of many years
slipped her mortal form,

he wept bitterly, of course,
but then was heard to say,

"Thank you, Mother Divine,
for my sweet and dearest wife.

My love for her has opened my heart
for loving you, the more."

ఴఴ

One day, a villager stopped and asked the man,

"Kind sir, why are you so grateful
at times when its least expected?"

The man smiled and replied,

"Ah, gratitude! The more you feel it,
the more reasons you have to feel it."

Then he continued on his way.

ఴఴ

One day, while traveling in the high mountains,
the earth suddenly shook beneath him.

From the summit of a tall mountain,
boulders began to break apart.
They rolled swiftly down the mountainside
crushing mighty trees
and all that stood before them.

When the boulders were but inches from his feet,
they suddenly and miraculously stopped.

The man turned to the mountain
and said, gratefully, "thank you,"
then continued on his way.

17

Nilla's Dearest Friend

Nilla's life was filled with rage;
so deep in her, it burned.
And like the fire, she kept it fed
to keep it growing strong.

Rage became her dearest friend;
it never left her side.
And all it ever asked of her
was to feed upon her heart.

Rage became her only love,
and vigilant protector;
a constant friend, and ever faithful,
loyal and never failing.

And through the years, as Nilla grew,
so, too, her dearest friend.

And all it ever asked of her
was to feed upon her heart.

෴

Her dearest friend taught Nilla well
how to navigate through life;
to sail alone in bitterness
on a sea of deadened dreams.

Since she viewed the world through
her dear friend's eyes,
all she saw she hated.

And all it ever asked of her
was to feed upon her heart.

෴

And feed it did till none was left
and Nilla's heart gave out.
Alone and bitter to the very end;
unwavering in her devotion.

Nilla gave her dearest friend
all she asked, and more.

෴

When Nilla left her mortal form,
much to her surprise,
waiting on the other side
was her dearest friend of all.

And all it will ever ask of her
is to feed upon her heart.

18

A Lesson on Believing You're Special

A teacher asked his students,
"Beloved children, who among you is special?"

All the children proudly raised their hands.

"Oh my!" replied the teacher.
"How can all of you be special?

If one of you is special,
there must be someone less.

So, what is it that makes you better?
What makes the other less?"

The children thought for a while,
but not one among them had an answer.

The teacher then told a story.

"A man journeyed to the
Hall of Self Awareness.
At the gate stood a tall sentinel
who asked him, 'Are you special?'

To which the man replied,
'Yes, sir. Indeed, I'm very special.'

'What makes you special?'
inquired the sentinel.

The man did not have an answer.

The guard frowned and said to the man,
'Go back from where you came.
This place is not for you.'

৪৩০৪

A second man came to the
Hall of Self Awareness.

The sentinel asked him,
'Are you special?'

To which he replied,
'Most certainly, sir! I'm very special.'

'What makes you special?'
inquired the sentinel.

The man did not have an answer.

The guard frowned and said to the man,
'Go back from where you came.
This place is not for you.'

෯෯

A third man came to the
Hall of Self Awareness.

The sentinel asked him,
'Are you special?'

The man replied with a laugh,
'Oh no, not at all,
but I am wonderfully unique.'

The guard smiled and said,
'Welcome, my friend.
This place is definitely for you.'

The man entered the Hall of Self Awareness.
There he discovered more of his uniqueness,
and more of his real self."

෯෯

The teacher then explained to the students,

"You see, my children, no one's special.
Specialness is arrogance.
It's a false belief that people have
in believing they're more or less.

No one is ever special,
but all are wonderfully unique.

So long as you believe you're special,
you'll never come to know
the beautiful uniqueness that is you,
and you alone."

In the Hall of Self Awareness,
very few get in.

19

The River

She was selling flowers by the river's edge.
He was walking with his friends.
He approached her and talked of little things.
She listened and thought them grand.

When he smiled at her, his eyes twinkled.
She blushed and fingered a lock of hair.

That was how they met.
And they loved each other ever since.

The river flows on to the sea.

Cords of light entwined their hearts,
woven by their Souls.
Their Spirits taught them the lover's dance
of ebbing and of flowing.

They walked through life by each other's side,
raised children, and made a home.

And though there were times of light and dark,
they weathered both with love.

And now and then, he would smile at her,
and his eyes would twinkle.
She would blush and finger a lock of hair.

❧

They grew old together,
but their love stayed young.

He was, to her, more handsome than ever.
She was, to him, never more beautiful.

With children grown,
and with families of their own,
they held each other closely
embracing the time they had together.

❧

As he lay dying,
he looked up at her and smiled;
a twinkle in his eye.
She blushed and fingered a lock
of silver hair.

The river becomes one with the sea.

❧

That was a hundred years ago.

❧

He was walking along the river's edge.
She was sitting with her friends.
He asked her the way to Sulimar.
She held him closely with her gaze.

When he smiled at her, his eyes twinkled.
She blushed and fingered a lock of hair.

And though they never met,
they recognized each other.

The sea becomes the river once again.

20

The Tale of the Chuckling Saint

By the banks of a gently flowing river
sat an old man and his granddaughter.

"Tell me a story, grandfather,"
said the young girl.

"Well, my child," began the old man,
"There was once a great saint
who sat beneath a tall mango tree.

It was said by all that this great saint
could perform miraculous feats,
though none had seen him do so.

One day, three young men sat before
the saint, chuckling amongst themselves.

'O' great Saint!' said the first youth,
'Perform a miracle for us. Fly in the air
if you can!'

The old saint just sat and chuckled.

'O' Illumined One!' said the second youth,
'Prove to us your enlightenment!
Make gold coins appear before us!'

The old saint just sat and chuckled.

'O' gifted Master!' said the third youth,
who could hardly keep from laughing,
'We beseech thee!
Make at least one miracle happen;
even a tiny, simple one!'

The old saint just sat and chuckled.

'Let's go,' spoke the first youth.
'There's no magic here. He's a fake.
And, besides, I'm getting hungry.'

They went to partake of a hardy meal,
laughing loudly as they went.

The old saint glanced up at the mango tree
and noticed on the highest branch
a ripe, tasty fruit.

His body floated in the air
to where the mango grew.

He picked the fruit,
gently descended like a feather
to the ground, ate the tasty mango,
then chuckled to himself."

᪥ᬑ

The young girl said to her grandfather,

"Why didn't the saint perform a miracle
for the three young men, grandfather?
That would have proven he was a great saint."

"Because, my dear," replied the old man,
"His greatness needed no proof.

Besides, they would never have believed
what their eyes had seen.

Miracles are best discovered on one's own,
my dear"

He chuckled.

21

Two Healings

An old woman lay at the edge of dying.

Just before she was to pass beyond,
she gazed out her window
and was awed by the beauty of the rising sun.

Although she'd seen this sight a thousand
times before,
this rising sun enchanted her.

It touched her soul so deeply,
that an enormous change happened within her.

She declared to herself,
"I will live."

And in time, the sickness passed.

She lived many more years, a more
enlightened woman.

An old woman lay at the edge of dying.

Just before she was to pass beyond,
she gazed out her window
and was awed by the beauty of the rising sun.

Although she'd seen this sight a thousand
times before,
this rising sun enchanted her.

It touched her soul so deeply,
that an enormous change happened within her.

She declared to herself,
"My loved ones will be fine. All is well.
I can leave peacefully now."

And, with a radiant smile, passed beyond;
a more enlightened woman.

ॐ

Such are the ways of healing.

22

The Path Maker

A disciple of a holy master asked his
beloved teacher,

"Great One, talk to us of the
'Path to Freedom'
and how we, your faithful disciples,
may know this blessed way."

The Master thought for a while,
then told a story.

෨෪

"Seven seekers journeyed in search of the
Path to Freedom.

When they came to the place where
the road ended,
they beheld an infinite array of paths
waiting before them.

෨෪

The Warrior took the
'Path of Heroic Struggle.'

And though he struggled faithfully his
entire life,
he died without finding freedom.

The Priest took the
'Path of the Sacred Texts.'

And though he lived a pious and saintly life,
he died without finding freedom.

The Lover took the
'Path of Love and Sacrifice.'

And though she loved all she knew,
and gave of all she had,
she died without finding freedom.

The Scholar took the
'Path of Knowledge.'

And though she learned all there was
to learn,
she died without finding freedom.

The Healer took the
'Path of Service.'

And though he tried to heal the world,
he died without finding freedom.

The Disciple took the
'Path of Devotion.'

And though he was faithful to his
beloved Master,
and obeyed his every word,
he died without finding freedom.

The Rebel took no path at all;
she made her own instead.

Since there was no map for her to follow,
for none had gone before,
she traveled alone through the vast unknown
and found what she was looking for:
Freedom."

"Enlightened One!"
cried the faithful disciples,

"You're our blessed 'Path to Freedom,'
our way-shower, our beloved guide,
and teacher!
We devote ourselves to you completely
and follow your every word
and deed faithfully."

"There's your mistake," scolded the Master.

"I'm only a friend along your path;
there to give support when asked,

and comfort when the way gets hard,
and a bit of counsel now and then.

But, mainly, I offer love.
More than that, no Master can do.

There's only one 'Path to Freedom,'
and that's the one you're on.

Be a rebel;
go and make your map."

23

Mohan at the Gate of Bliss

Mohan was the most feared
and evil of souls.

He took great pleasure in ending lives,
and relished in the suffering
and destruction he caused.

Many lifetimes came and went,
yet Mohan grew not in compassion,
or remorse.

Indeed, he was the evilest of souls.

So, when the Old One,
the Keeper of the Gate of Bliss,
asked the soul of Mohan,

"Choose my son; enter or remain."

Mohan laughed his evil laugh and said,
"You must be mad, Old One!

I, Mohan, pass through the Gate of Bliss?
I, Mohan, the Destroyer,
whose karma is the weight of a thousand stars?
I, Mohan, the most evil of men,
enter the realm of eternal peace and bliss?

Be warned, Old One; do not mock me!"
Then he stormed away into another
incarnation.

Again, and again, after each lifetime,
Mohan would find himself before the
Gate of Bliss.
And again, and again, the Old One would say,

"Choose my son; enter or remain."

And Mohan's answer would always be
the same.

"Be warned, Old One; do not mock me!"
Then he'd storm away into another
incarnation.

Yet all beings shall pass one day
through the Gate of Bliss;
for this is the promise of Divine Mother.

Mohan is no exception.

ೞೞ

And the day came.

ೞೞ

Mohan stood before the Old One,
the Keeper of the Gate of Bliss,
filled with deep remorse
for all the evil deeds he'd done.

"Old One, I am the greatest of fools!"
he cried,
"For I have wasted a thousand lifetimes
in acts of rage and evil!

My karma is so great,
I fear I shall never pass beyond the
Gate of Bliss!"

Mohan fell to his knees
and wept with sincerity and depth.

The Old One knelt beside him
and held him lovingly in her arms.

To the pitiful Mohan, she whispered
these words.

"My son, there is no karma. There never was.
Retribution is a human folly;
never apart of Divine Mother's love.

You could have entered the Gate of Bliss
at any time by simply walking through.
Your rage, dear one, blinded you to this.

So, I ask again, enter or remain?"

The weight of a million pains lifted from Mohan,
and he radiated with celestial brilliance
as he entered the Gate of Bliss;
laughing and weeping into the awaiting arms of
Divine Mother.

ॐ

Since Mohan was the last to enter
the Gate of Bliss,
the Old One turned off the light,
shut the gate behind her,
and returned to the Realm of Forgiveness.

24

Rumesh Pays Respect

The Master lay on his bed, dying.
All about him were his devoted followers
weeping bitterly.

Rumesh, on the other hand,
sat in a mango grove
playing his wooden flute.

When the Master died, his devoted followers
anointed his body in fragrant oil
and clothed him in the finest silk.

And for three days, and three nights,
as was the custom,
they knelt before his lifeless body
chanting and weeping bitterly.

Rumesh, on the other hand,
sat in a mango grove
playing his wooden flute.

On the fourth day, as was the custom,
they placed his body on the funeral pyre
and covered him in white petals.
All wept bitterly
at the loss of their beloved Master.

Rumesh, on the other hand,
sat in a mango grove
playing his wooden flute.

They sprinkled white petals on his
lifeless form, as was the custom,
then covered him in kindling sticks.
They set ablaze the funeral pyre,
then wept bitterly as his body turned to ash.

Rumesh, on the other hand,
sat in a mango grove
playing his wooden flute.

They took the ashes to the holy river
and cast them upon the sacred water,
then, one by one, bid a tearful farewell
as the ashes journeyed on to the sea.

All who gathered threw white petals
upon the water, as was the custom.

Rumesh, on the other hand,
sat in a mango grove
playing his wooden flute.

ဆၣႢ

The others, sorely angered by
Rumesh's absence,
said nothing out of respect for their
beloved Master.
But, now that he was gone,
they decided to confront him
to express their great displeasure.

"Rumesh, why did you show such
disrespect to your beloved Master?"
they cried out in anger.

"He had given you his love,
and this is how you pay respect?"

Rumesh calmly replied,
"Master is not dead to me.
What loss is there to mourn?

Once Master was with me in the flesh,
but now he's with me more.
Weep not for his life that was,
but celebrate his life now living in you
forever.

Love grows all the stronger
when you can let it go."

Then, from a clear blue sky,
thousands of petals fell
and blanketed all in white.

The others wept with joy
at this wondrous sight.

Rumesh, on the other hand, closed his eyes
and played his Master's favorite tune
on his wooden flute.

25

The Saint Who Loved Science

A great saint, the wisest of all the saints,
sat beneath a willow tree
expounding on the wonders of science,
and extolling its many virtues.

Among the multitude of his devoted followers
sat three priests of the
High and Holy Temple.

As the saint spoke on and on of the miracles
of science,
they became so perplexed
they could sit in silence no longer.

"O' Great One,"
interrupted the first priest.

"Why do you speak so fondly of science,
and all its many virtues?
Science will never discover God."

"It's true what you say," replied the saint.

"In seeking to capture the eternal
within the finite mind,
science will never achieve its goal,
but at least, dear one, it's trying."

ॐ

"O' Great One,"
interrupted the second priest.

"Is it not true that man finds God in the
sanctity of religious life?"

"It may be true for some," replied the saint.

"You may find God within religious practice,
but you'll never find religion in God.

Spirituality is a private journey to discover
the more of you.

God is found along the journey;
and the journey is forever.
Science, in its search for God,
is undoubtedly on that journey."

ॐ

O' Great One!"
interrupted the third priest.

"As priests well versed in the Sacred Texts,
and prayerful every day,
are we not closer to the grace of God
then science for all its searching?"

"Oh, my!" exclaimed the saint.

"Better to be a humble scientist who seeks,
then an arrogant priest who foolishly thinks
he's arrived."

26

The Two Lovers
Who Never Met

She was all he ever hoped for.
He was the man of her dreams.
And in the dreaming of their nights,
they'd lie together in love's embrace,
though these lovers never met.

He would listen for her in every woman's voice.
She would look in every man's eyes
to see if he looked back.
And though many times they fell in love,
it was never the love they yearned for,
the lover they never met.

The love they felt for one another
is the most powerful of loves.
It comes when souls unite two hearts
in the euphoric dance of one.

When they married,
and thought they finally found

their one and only love,
deep inside, well-hidden, they knew
it was not the lover they forever sought.

ဆၢ

They'll search for each other all their lives,
and for many lives to come.

And when all he loves about her
he finds within himself,
and when she no longer needs him,
then, and only then,
will these two lovers meet.

27

The Answer is Always "Yes"

Eight pilgrims gathered by a forest pool
on a journey to the High Temple.

After they ate their meal and quenched
their thirst,
Goddess, the Divine Mother,
appeared before them
radiant in her luminescence.

"Ask me what you will," Goddess spoke,
"and I shall surely grant it."

ഇന്റെ

The first pilgrim bowed low and said,
"I wish to struggle, and toil, and suffer,
as proof of my devotion."

"Yes,"
Goddess answered, sadly.

ഇന്റെ

The second pilgrim bowed low and said,
"I wish to blame you for all the ills, and pains,
and failures of my life."

"Yes,"
Goddess answered, sadly.

The third pilgrim bowed low and said,
"I desire to be a loser in the living of my life,
wallowing in my self-pity."

"Yes,"
Goddess answered, sadly.

The fourth pilgrim bowed low and said,
"I desire to hold tightly to my rage and bitterness,
and my ceaseless war with thee."

"Yes,"
Goddess answered, sadly.

The fifth pilgrim bowed low and said,
"I desire a life free of struggle, toil, and suffering
as proof of my devotion."

"Oh, yes!"
Goddess answered with delight.

The sixth pilgrim bowed low and said,
"I desire to take responsibility for all the ills,
and pains, and failures of my life
that I may grow from them and forgive myself."

"Oh, yes!"
Goddess answered with delight.

The seventh pilgrim bowed low and said,
"I desire to be a winner in the living of my life;
happy and joyfully free."

"Oh, yes!"
Goddess answered with delight.

The eighth pilgrim bowed low and said,
"I desire to be free of rage and bitterness,
and to dance with thee forever."

"Oh, yes! Oh, yes!"
Goddess answered with great delight.

You see, Goddess answers "*yes*"
to all that you request.
It's because she loves you so.

'*Choice*' is her gift to you, dear one,
and she'll never take it back.

Oh, and you should also know,
her patience is unending.

ഇരു

So, what are you requesting?

The answer is always "yes."

28

In the Fire of the Muse

A painter came to a sacred grotto.

Before the grotto, a roaring fire,
and beside it stood one of the nine radiant
Sisters of the Muse.

"I seek creativity," declared the painter.

The goddess replied,
"And what is the price you're willing to pay?"

To which the painter replied,
"I give you all I hold of martyr
with its false belief in sacrifice."

The goddess lifted him
and tossed him into the flames,
and the fire consumed him.

In time, he became a most beloved painter
whose art burst forth in divine light and color.

ೞಓಞ

A musician came to the sacred grotto.

"I seek creativity," he declared.

The goddess replied,
"And what is the price you're willing to pay?"

To which the musician replied,
"I give you all my need for validation,
and my desperate search for vindication."

The goddess lifted him
and tossed him into the flames,
and the fire consumed him.

In time, he became a most beloved composer
whose music filled souls and spirits
with divine and rapturous sounds.

ೞಓಞ

A philosopher came to the sacred grotto.

"I seek creativity," he declared.

The goddess replied,
"And what is the price you're willing to pay?"

To which the philosopher replied,
"I give you all my arrogance
with its false promise of specialness."

The goddess lifted him
and tossed him into the flames,
and the fire consumed him.

In time, he became a most learned sage
whose wisdom inspired all
to aspire to the divine of love.

৩০৪

A poet came to the sacred grotto.

"I seek creativity," he declared.

The goddess replied,
"And what is the price you're willing to pay?"

The poet thought long and hard,
then replied,

"I'll give you half of my advance
plus 10% of sales for the first year,
then 7.5 each year after that."

The goddess lifted him
and tossed him into the flames,
and the fire consumed him.

In time, he became a relatively adequate
writer of limericks.

৩০৪

The moral of our story, dear friends:
'You don't want to mess with an archetype.'

29

What a Rare and Special Child!

The disciples sat before their beloved Master.

One woman stood up before him and announced,
"O' great and beloved Master, I'm indeed blessed.
Oh, how God has blessed me!

I'm most fortunate to be the mother
of a rare and special child."

The disciples murmured among themselves.
In complete agreement were they
as to the magnificence of the child.

☜☞

"By the age of three," she continued,
"my most rare and special child
gained the wisdom, and mastered
the knowledge
of all the ancient holy teachings.

Now at the age of nine,
he recites the Sacred Texts
without missing a single word,
and he does it all with perfect tone
and inflection."

A chubby little boy of nine enlightened years
stood up beside his mother
and recited several sacred verses
without missing a single word;
and with perfect tone and inflection.

The Master sat silently nodding his head,
a smile upon his face.

The disciples murmured among themselves.
In complete agreement were they
as to the magnificence of the child.

ॐ

"O' great and beloved Master,"
the mother continued on,
"And you should hear him sing!
Not one among the Celestial Chorus
can match him for its beauty!"

The chubby little boy of nine enlightened years,
standing beside his adoring mother,
sang out in a most beautiful voice,
a sound worthy of the divine Celestial Chorus.

The Master sat silently nodding his head,
a smile upon his face.

The disciples murmured among themselves.
In complete agreement were they
as to the magnificence of the child.

The mother went on and on
for what seemed to be an hour,
extolling the unlimited wonders
of her rare and special child.

After a time,
the Master glanced down at the chubby
little boy seated beside his gushing mother
and noticed the child picking his nose
while staring blankly off into nothingness.

The Master let out a loud and hardy laugh.

"Oh, yes, I can see indeed,
a most rare and special child!"

30

The Secret Teaching

A woman hungered for the
Ultimate Truth.

So desirous of this was she
that she gave up all her possessions
and wandered the earth for forty years
in search of a master who could teach her.

She journeyed high into the sacred mountains
and deep into the Valley of the Saints.

She knelt before the greatest teachers,
but none could satisfy her hunger
to find the Ultimate Truth.

She traveled distant plains and deserts,
and into dark and forbidding forests.

She studied the teachings of a thousand
sacred traditions,
but none could satisfy her hunger
to find the Ultimate Truth.

Though she suffered many hardships,
and endured much loss and pain,
she never gave up in her pursuit
to find an illumined master
who could teach her the Ultimate Truth.

Then one day,
she found what she, for a lifetime, sought.

High in the remotest of mountains,
deep in a mountain cave,
the most illumined of illumined masters
sat in deep meditation.

Kneeling at the Master's lotus feet,
she humbly beseeched him,

"O' great and most radiant of Masters,
I beg thee.
Impart to me the Secret Teaching
that I, too,
may know the Ultimate Truth.

The great Sage sat in silence
for a very, very long time.

Then, as the sun slowly descended
behind the western mountains,
the great Sage spoke.

ॐ

"Eat your vegetables."

ॐ

The woman sat for many days
deeply absorbed in thought.

Then a smile shone upon her face
and grew radiant like the sun.

She knew!

Her eyes began to sparkle
like a thousand twinkling stars,
and a soft glow flowed
from her awakened heart,
illuminating the dark of night.

She found peace.
She was adrift in bliss.
She was free.

She found the Ultimate Truth.

31

Kotia and the Bawdy Woman

Kotia was a most respectable woman.

She only said the nicest things
and always acted in utmost propriety.

She never lowered herself to anger,
or swore, or raised her voice.
And she never, ever laughed out loud,
but offered, instead, a smile.

Yes,
Kotia was the most appropriate of women.

One day, while walking gracefully
along a country lane,
Kotia came upon a most crude
and vulgar woman.

She wore brightly colored clothing,
none of which matched,

and spit, and swore, and laughed out loud
with such abandon
everyone near got sprayed
with yucky spittle.

Kotia looked down with disgust at this vile
and bawdy woman,
and thought it most appropriate
to steal away quietly
in the opposite direction.

But she hesitated.

There was something about this buxom,
roughhewn woman,
whose makeup looked as if applied
with strokes of a house painters brush,
something that held her in rapt attention.
A feeling stirred inside her,
a deep and hidden feeling.
She sensed an ancient yearning,
a yearning for such freedom.

So, Kotia and the woman started talking
and soon became close friends.
And, over time, the bawdy woman
taught Kotia the 'Bawdy Way.'

The teaching, of course, was one-sided,
for there was nothing about Kotia
the bawdy woman wanted,
other than her friendship.

Her friend taught Kotia how to spit
and laugh out loud;
the kind of laugh that comes from deep
inside the belly.

And she taught Kotia the secrets
of applying makeup
by splashing it all over the face.
The bawdy woman loved makeup so.

And she taught Kotia how to pinch a bottom,
and to be honest with her heart.

She taught Kotia how to swear
and speak most inappropriately.
And if people did not like it,
she taught Kotia
how to slap them on the ass.

But, most of all,
Kotia learned from her bawdy friend
how to be a woman honest to herself;
a woman wild and free.

In time, Kotia became a bawdy woman,
open, alive, and loving.

And if she met a man she thought was cute,
she had no problem pinching him in the ass.

But only if she wanted to.

32

Bindu at the End of the World

The Great Seer came down from his
mountain cave
to proclaim what he had seen.

People gathered from far and wide
to hear him speak,
for never once were his predictions wrong.

"Prepare your selves," he bellowed.
"The world will end in seven days!"

Great fear and chaos spread throughout
the land.
Men and women, young and old,
terror gripped them all.

"The end of the world is coming!
The end of the world is coming!"
they cried,

and fell to the ground weeping
and quivering with dread.

Except for Bindu.

Bindu did what Bindu does.
He daydreamed wonderful things.

☙❧

Those of wealth and stature
gave all they had to the poor
in hopes of gaining favor in the afterlife.

Those of note and position
climbed the highest mountains
to be the first taken into Heaven.

Those of intelligence and learning
dug deep holes in the ground
to escape the inevitable destruction.

Those of divine grace and countenance
huddled in the holy temples convinced that
Divine Mother would never harm them there.

And the rest just went on with their lives,
oblivious to all around them.

But not Bindu.

Bindu did what Bindu does.
He daydreamed wonderful things.

☙❧

On the seventh day, all was still and quiet.

Bindu sat beneath his banyan tree
daydreaming
when along came Divine Mother.

Bindu woke from his dreaming,
and when he saw Divine Mother,
he exclaimed,
"Beloved Mother!
How wonderful it is to see you!"

"Oh, my beloved Bindu,"
said Divine Mother,

"Today the old-world ends,
today the new begins!
Come, Bindu, help me deliver my gift."

Divine Mother opened her heart
and a great awakening
flooded the world with light, and hope,
and dreams.

She soaked everything in
glistening mists of enchantment,
and all became awash
in unbridled imagination and wonder,
and the world sparkled and shined
like a newborn child.

Bindu added a few dreams of his own.

The day after the world ended,
those of wealth and stature
frantically tried to get back
all they had graciously given away.

Those of note and position
scurried down from the highest mountains,
feeling quite humiliated.

Those of intelligence and learning
scrambled from their burrows beneath
the ground,
leaving behind provisions just in case.

Those of divine grace and countenance
proudly descended from the holy temples
convinced that all were saved by the fervor
of their prayers.

And the rest just went on with their lives
oblivious to all around them.

And Bindu?

Well, Bindu did what Bindu does.
He daydreamed wonderful things.

හායෙ

No one noticed the old-world gone
and the birthing of the new,
not yet.

But, Bindu did.

33

Martyr's Many Lifetimes

She was a most accomplished martyr,
which is not surprising
since she practiced it diligently every day.

And she always made sure she had
an audience
when performing the martyr's ritual
of silent suffering,
and feeling unloved and unappreciated.

Suffering was her prized possession;
it was her
Martyr's Badge of Love.

She selfishly sacrificed everything
for those she loved and cared for,
but never once did she realize
the price she made them pay.

If no one acknowledged the pain she felt,
she would go off by herself,
and heave and sigh, and weep alone,
and feel unloved and unappreciated.

Suffering was her prized possession;
it was her
Martyr's Badge of Love.

ℬℭ

As is the case with all such martyrs,
she never realized how much she loved it,
or the false power it made her feel,
or how addicted she had become
to its sweet intoxication.

And, as is the way with all such martyrs,
if anyone offered love to her,
she would go off by herself,
and heave and sigh,
and grow red with rage.

How dare someone upstages her!

For suffering was her prized possession;
it was her
Martyr's Badge of Love.

And it was, most of all, hers and hers alone!

ℬℭ

Such was the life of this martyred woman,
and for a thousand lives to come.

And not once, in all those thousand lifetimes,
did she come to realize
how much she truly loved it.

And if anyone brought it to her attention,
she would go off by herself,
and heave and sigh,
and weep alone,
and feel unloved and unappreciated.

Suffering was her prized possession;
it was her
Martyr's Badge of Love.

శుభం

But, after many lifetimes
devoted to her martyr,
she finally came to realize
how much she truly loved it,
and how sweet the intoxication
martyrdom became.

And she hated herself for it.

So, she decided to pay attention
to her addiction.

శుభం

When she caught herself in martyr,
she made a different choice;
to forgive herself for holding on,
and to simply let it go.

And over time, bit by bit,
her martyr dissolved away.

Oh, she may slip up now and then,
and do a little martyr here and there.

But, for the most part, she's moved beyond,
and has come to realize how much she's loved,
and greatly appreciated.

Oh, and by the way,
she threw away her prized possession, her
Martyr's Badge of Love.

Now she started loving,
and now she started caring,
and now she started being happy.

ഇറ

Some people are just slow learners.

34

Three Old Women

There lived three old women,
so different in many ways.

The first, dreading old age,
chose never to grow up.

The second, welcoming her age,
knew the secrets of the Ancient Ones.

And the third, well,
she just stared out her window,
counted the passersby,
and waited to die.

The first, desperate for love,
tried to find it
by becoming a teenager once again.

The second, knowing she's loved,
graciously shared the love
with others.

And the third, well,
she just stared out her window,
counted the passersby,
and waited to die.

࿐

The first, searching for happiness,
looked for it in things long dead.

The second, knowing happiness,
danced naked in the woods.

And the third, well,
she just stared out her window,
counted the passersby,
and waited to die.

࿐

The first, when others talked,
interrupted and said,
"I remember the time when…"

The second, when others talked,
listened with genuine interest.

And the third, well,
when others talked, she didn't hear them.
She just stared out her window,

counted the passersby,
and waited to die.

The first, when looking at her life,
saw failed dreams and lost hopes.

The second, when looking at her life,
saw her power flourish.

And the third stopped looking a long
time ago;
for she saw only passersby
outside her window.

She died.

The first old woman: The Silly Old Fool.

The second old woman: The Wise One.

And the third old woman, well,
she has no name.

She lost it a long time ago.

35

Gopol Talks to God

Gopol did not attend the Holy Temple,
much to the dismay of the temple priest.

He was not pious like the others in his village.

And during the High Days of
Holy Observance,
instead of fasting and worshiping
in God's Holy Temple,
he went fishing,
much to the dismay of the temple priest.

He did not like being in the Holy Temple.
He found the seats too hard,
the chants too dull,
and the Sacred Texts
too hard to understand.

He preferred, instead, to lie
in a soft green meadow
singing nonsense songs to the clouds,

and to write poems about dandelions
and gypsy moths,
much to the dismay of the temple priest.

෴

One day, the temple priest,
while strolling through the wood,
came upon a ring of seven trees,
and there within sat
Gopol talking with God.

They chatted away like old friends
and laughed like silly children.
They sometimes danced like
intoxicated lovers,
and sometimes picked berries
from a nearby bush.

The temple priest, outraged,
ran back to the Holy Temple,
fell to his knees before
the Holy Statue of God,
and prayed for the soul of Gopol,

much to the dismay of God.

36

The Actor Assumes His Role

The playwright could not find an actor
to play the leading role.

Since he wrote the play and knew the lines,
he decided to play the role himself.

The play ran every day and night
for as long as he could remember,
and he always had an audience
to act his play before.

He played the role so very well,
the audience thought it true,
and over time the playwright, too,
believed the play was real.

And over time, he forgot himself
and became a made-up role.
He became the leading character
in a play of his own creation.

Although the play was never real,
its lines became his words.
And although the play was never real,
its story became his life.

And all the made-up tragedies,
and all the comedies too,
became real events in a fantasy world
he sadly believed was true.

The play took such a toll him,
he decided he needed help
in healing the pains and tragedies
of this life that wasn't real.

So, he sought the guidance of a sage
who could help him in his plight.

"My dear friend," said the Sage,
"All of what you're living, none of it is true.
Your life's a story your mind made up,
and your belief is making real.

You're not wrong or bad, my son,
in believing what you do.
You're just mistaken, that is all,
in believing what you're not.

Awaken to who you truly are,
the author of your play,

and write a life that best reflects
the realness in you."

൭൜

The Sage helped him, step by step,
to awaken from his dream.
And slowly and steadily, over time,
the playwright came to realize
that he, and only he,
is the author of his play.

And slowly and steadily, over time,
he also came to realize,
it's always in the author's power
to write any play he wished.

൭൜

"What is your play, my friend?

Do you like it? If not, rewrite it."

37

The Greatest Gift

A Master sat beneath the cooling shade
of an ancient Grandfather Tree,
his beloved disciples before him.

"What is the greatest gift you can give to
Divine Mother?" he asked.

They thought awhile,
some silently, some among themselves.

The Keeper of the Trees
spoke first.

"The greatest gift would be a
loving family.

With its branches spreading wide
to encompass all within its love.
A family with roots deep and strong
to keep it standing

even in the fiercest storm."

☙❧

The Mighty Warrior
spoke next.

"The greatest gift is the gift of
compassion.

To be the champion of those less fortunate,
and to uphold the dignity of all."

☙❧

The Mother
was next to speak.

"The greatest gift is the gift of
children.

Children who grow to fine adults,
honoring and loving themselves.
Children strong enough to love,
and stronger still to receive it."

☙❧

Two Lovers
now took their turn.

"The greatest gift is the gift of
love,
along with committed practice.

To be in the intoxicating embrace of love,
is to dance with Mother Divine."

❧

The Merchant
now spoke.

"The greatest gift is the gift of
a *rich and abundant life*.

A life overflowing with fulfilling successes,
and failures from which we grow."

❧

The Poet
was last to speak.

"The greatest gift is the gift of
creativity.

To leave something of yourself behind
that makes the world a better place
for your having been upon it."

❧

The Master lay back against
the Grandfather Tree
and took from his cloak a mango.

Gazing longingly at the ripened fruit,
he spoke.

"All of the gifts you speak of
are beautiful gifts to give,
but they're not the greatest gift.

Divine Mother gifted you
Life,
and free choice in which to live it.

The greatest gift to her
is to learn to receive her gift,
and in that life,
Enjoy."

&

He took a large bite from the awaiting mango,
the sweet juice flowing freely down his beard.

He gave a tiny burp, then smiled,
and rested beneath the Grandfather Tree,
contented.

38

Thirty Days in the Infinite

A great sage sat for thirty days,
and thirty nights,
in the deepest contemplation,
his inner eye steady upon the Infinite.

Adrift was he in unbounded truth,
and at one with eternal bliss.

And all the while his faithful disciples
knelt lovingly before him,
basking in his divine presence.

ॐ

Then,
on the thirtieth night, of the thirtieth day,
he opened his dreamy eyes
and gazed out at an awaiting world.

ॐ

"We beg thee, O' Bringer of Light!"
his disciples cried out,
"Alone in the darkness of ignorance,
we seek the light of your infinite knowledge!"

"O' divine Teacher,"
they cried out again,
"We thirst for the waters of your wisdom!"

"O' exalted Master,"
begged the disciples even more,
"We're starving for the divine fruits from the
infinite tree of bliss!

Speak, O' Blessed One!

Speak, O' Great Seer of the Divine!

Speak, we beg thee, speak!"

The great illumined Master blissfully smiled,
then spoke to the gathered multitude
in a solemn, ethereal voice.

"I have to take a pee."

39

Sundeep and the Simple Life

Oh, how Sundeep yearned for the simple life,
and the simple times, and the simple ways!

"Why must everything be so hard?"
He would often say.

"Our lives would be much easier
if we lived a simple life!"

One day, Sundeep, tired of this complex world,
bought fifteen chickens and one large cow,
and gathered what he could carry,
and went to live in the remotest part
of the remotest forest
in the remotest region of the land.

He built a modest hut of sticks and mud
by a gently flowing stream,
and settled down for a rustic life,

a simple life,
free of complications.

"Ah!" he said to himself, contented.
"Now, I shall live a simple, peaceful life,
free of complications!"

But living the simple life was not
what he imagined.

୫୦ରେ

He would rise each morning before the sun
to milk his only cow,
then gather eggs, feed his hens,
and collect water from the stream.

During the early break of dawn,
he ground the corn and pounded wheat,
and baked the bread for his daily meal.

He would work throughout the morning
tilling his tiny field with a hoe, he made by hand,
and would stop only when he could work
no more, or his hands began to bleed.

After a meager lunch,
he would take his soiled clothes
to the gently flowing stream
to beat them on the rocks.

He beat and soaked, and beat and soaked,
till they were somewhat clean.

Throughout the afternoon, he made the tools,
and crafted the pots,
and built and repaired the many things
he would need in the course of
day to day living the rustic, simple life.

At night he made some candles
by the glow of candlelight,
then, aching in pain and full of exhaustion,
retired to his sleep
on a small, hard wooden cot.

␚

Every day, and every night,
for months and months on end,
Sundeep did his many chores,
and performed his many tasks,
to live the simple life.

And, although he had no time to complain,
every now and then,
in those rare and precious moments
when he had the time to think,
he thought of his days in the village
and would yearn
for the complex life.

40

The King of Beasts

One day,
the elders of all the beasts of the earth
gathered in counsel to choose the
The King of Beasts.

ဆင

The Lion was first to speak on his behalf.

"All gathered here
know me to be the mightiest of the beasts.

As King of Beasts
I'll serve as a protector and guardian to all;
for the world is much in need
of a champion of the weak."

ဆင

The next to speak on her behalf was
the Lamb.

"All gathered here
know me to be the gentlest of the beasts.

As King of Beasts
I'll love and nurture all;
for the world is much in need
of love and kindness."

☙❧

Now spoke the Hawk.

"All gathered here
know me to be the loftiest of the beasts.

As King of Beasts
I'll be a visionary finding futures that soar
with light;
for the world is much in need
of hope and dreams."

☙❧

Then spoke the tiny Ant.

"All gathered here
know me to be the most industrious
of the beasts.

As King of Beasts
I'll work in partnership with all,
for the benefit of all;
for the world is much in need
of one who can shoulder enormous burdens."

ॐ

The Whale spoke on his behalf.

"All gathered here
know me to be the most ancient of the beasts.

As King of Beasts
I'll bring knowledge and wise counsel;
for the world is much in need
of the wisdom of the Ancients."

ॐ

Then spoke the colorful Peacock.

"All gathered here
know me to be the most beautiful of the beasts.

As King of Beasts
I'll bring grace and elegance;
for the world is much in need
of beauty and enchantment."

ॐ

Many more beasts spoke that day,
and presented their cases before the elders.

When all was said and done,
the elders gathered together
and made their decision.

ॐ

"Who would you choose, beloved?

I'm curious. Why?"

41

A Legitimate Profession

One day, a man sat upon the ground
and immediately found himself
in excruciating pain.

In such pain was he
that he sought the care and treatment
of the three most renowned doctors in the land.

The three doctors examined the man
thoroughly,
and after much consultation and deliberation,
the first doctor spoke.

"There's no doubt in my mind
that this poor man is suffering from acute
Under Overberger Syndrome,
or UOS as it's commonly called."

"I'm sorry, my dear colleague,"
said the second doctor,
"I must politely disagree.

He shows all the signs of stage twelve
Kakapepeosis."

The third doctor shook his head and sighed.

"My dear colleagues,
having attended a conference recently
featuring the learned and most esteemed
Dr. I. M. Butkic,
of the University of Grungipore,
I have concluded, based on Dr. Butkic's
extensive research and findings,
that this gentleman suffers from a rear
and potentially lethal strain of
Inflammatory Woe Meningitis,
or IWM as it's commonly called."

While the three renowned doctors
debated the man's condition,
a cleaning wallah,
who was previously engaged in the cleaning
of an assortment of knives and thongs,
approached the groaning patient and lovingly
stroked his head,
which much comforted him.

It was then that the lowly cleaning wallah
made a startling discovery.

"Sirs!" exclaimed the wallah,
"This man has a thistle in his rump!"

After further consultation and much
deliberation,
the first doctor spoke.

"We must prop up this man immediately
so he can talk about his past,
especially about his mother."

After further consultation and much
deliberation,
the second doctor spoke.

"I suggest we remove his organs
and clean them nice and neat.
Then let's paint them a pretty color
and put them back again;
this usually does the trick."

After further consultation and much
deliberation,
the third doctor spoke.

"I suggest we give him daily injections
of sodium venomite, a highly lethal toxin.
Although these injections kill 99.9% of patients,

what harm can it do?
And it's been thoroughly tested
and approved."

∞

The cleaning wallah sat alone in the corner
pulling out his hair.

"But, Sirs!" he pleaded,
"He has a thistle in his rump!"

∞

After further consultation and much
deliberation,
the first doctor spoke.

"The best prognosis from my diagnosis:
The patient will need to meet me once a week
to talk about his mother.
Perhaps in twenty years, or more,
we'll see a slight improvement."

∞

After further consultation and much
deliberation,
the second doctor spoke.

"The best prognosis from my diagnosis:
The patient will have two to three weeks
to live at best.
I suggest knocking him out
to make him feel more comfortable."

After further consultation and much
deliberation,
the third doctor spoke.

"He should be dead by now.
Did anyone get his insurance number?"

And all the while, the cleaning wallah
sat alone in the corner, pulling out his hair.

"But, Sirs!" he pleaded,
"He has a thistle in his rump!"

While the renown doctors continued their
consultations and deliberations,
the cleaning wallah gently removed the thistle
from the dying man's rump,
which resulted in the man's full
and immediate recovery.

The man lived a long and happy life,
and made a particular point
of never sitting on thistles.

As to the cleaning wallah?

ॐ

He continued to do what he always did:
polish bones,
dust off the many tomes of medical knowledge,
clean blood and googies off the floor,
and every now and then,
heal a few people

(when the doctors weren't looking)

ॐ

Healing's not that hard
if you know where to look.

42

A Tale of Two Villages

While on a holy pilgrimage, a great Sage stopped
at a small village for refreshment.

The villagers gave him food and drink
and, in return,
asked the Sage to impart to them
the refreshment of his wisdom.

When the old Sage finished his meal,
the villagers gathered around to hear
him speak.

"There were two villages," began the Sage.

"The first village placed great value
on hard work and struggle.
So highly prized was hard work and struggle,
that when two villagers greeted one another
they would always say,

'Greetings, my friend. You're looking tired.
Are you working hard?'

To which the other would reply,

'Oh, most certainly! I'm working very,
very hard, and you?'

The other would respond the same.

This gave everyone assurance
that their lives were being lived as it should be.

Hard work was the highest virtue;
struggle, the highest merit,
and a place closest to God
to those who suffered most.

Children learned from an early age
that success belonged to those who worked,
and labored and struggled.

Mothers were honored above all others
for a life of toil and sacrifice.

And fathers?

They proved their love for family
through long hours of work and absence.

Though all in this village died
long before their time,
they believed eternal bliss,
and blessed rest,
awaited them in the afterlife."

ॐ

The Sage continued.

"The second village, on the other hand,
placed great value on happiness
and living a comfortable and elegant life.

So highly prized was happiness and ease,
that when two villagers greeted one another
they would always say,

'Greetings, my friend. You're looking happy.
Are you having fun?'

To which the other would reply,

'Oh, most certainly!
I'm enjoying myself very, very much,
and you?'

The other would respond the same.

This gave everyone assurance
that their lives were being lived as it should be.

Enjoying life was the highest virtue;
synchronous living, the highest merit,
and blissfully dancing with God
to those who worked hard or not.

Children learned from an early age
that success
belonged to those who crafted their lives
consciously, and had fun doing so.

Mothers were honored for teaching
their young that play should be forever.

And fathers?

They proved their love for family
through long hours of playing with their children,
and teaching them how to have adventures.

And all in this village lived long lives
filled with health, peace, and happiness."

౸౸

The great Sage ended his story
with a question.

"Which village would you rather be,
my friends?"

The villagers gathered around
and talked among themselves.

When they finished,
a tall, burly man stood up and said,

"We'd rather be the first village.
Being happy takes far too much hard work."

43

The Captain and the Sea

"Stay on course, and don't look back,
no matter the seas before you,"
said the
Captain to the Mate.

"Be the Captain of your ship, and sail her well
and true.

If your seas be rough, or your seas be calm,
be there wind, or none at all,
keep your bow ahead of you
till you're safely home to port.

You'll never sail alone, my boy,
you've a billion stars above you.
They'll guide you safely home, my lad,
if you'll allow yourself to trust them.

When rough seas come,
as they surely will,
take your sails in
and head her to the storm.

Don't run from storms, my lad,
but sail your ship ahead.
On the other side are better seas
and a calmer passage through.

And when you reach the other side,
as you will surely do,
unfurl your sails high and wide
and run her swift and true."

❧

"Now, know you this, and know you well,"
said the
Captain to the Mate,

"When your seas be rough, and your
sailing hard,
find the nearest port.
There'll always be safe harbors near
to refit and rest awhile.

And know you this, and know you well.
Keep the adventure in the voyage,
but take not the sea for granted.

Sail free, sail wise,
my fine young lad,
and never give up command.

And know you this, and know you well.

When your ship gets old beyond repair,
and can sail the seas no more,

calmly sail her to the next safe port
and exchange her for another.

You've a thousand seas before you, lad,
and a thousand ships to sail,
and a thousand adventures lie ahead
that eagerly await you,"

said the
Captain to the Mate.

44

An Abandoned Garden

She was the most hated in her village;
this vile, bitter woman.

She treated all with loathing and contempt,
and they all despised her for it.

She shunned all conversation
and avoided human contact,
and lived alone in a ramshackle hut
on the outskirts of the town.

When she left her darkened sanctum,
and she very seldom did,
people looked away from her
to avoid her hate-filled gaze.

No one in the village spoke to her,
she would never let them near;
but when she spoke, and she seldom did,

words spewed forth like acid
burning those close enough to hear.

Children thought her an evil witch,
and out of fright would run from sight
whenever she'd draw near;
but the older ones, to prove their courage,
would hide in her yard at night,
not daring to be seen.

One day, while walking to the village,
the old woman came upon a dying squirrel
lying in pain along the road.

She sat beside the suffering beast
and placed it in her lap,
then gently stroked the dying squirrel
until it passed from life.

She took the lifeless body
and buried it behind her darkened home
in a place overgrown with weeds and vines;
her once beloved and long-abandoned garden.

45

The Purpose of Life

Early one morning, before the break of dawn,
an old man and his young grandson
sat facing one another.

The old man gazed into the young boy's eyes
and chanted softly,

"The purpose of life is to enjoy.
The purpose of life is to enjoy.
The purpose of life is to enjoy."

After a long pause,
the young boy repeated the chant.

"The purpose of life is to enjoy.
The purpose of life is to enjoy.
The purpose of life is to enjoy."

The young boy
prided himself on his many toys
and playthings.

He thought to himself,
"I'm enjoying."

❧

In time, the child became an adolescent,
and prided himself on his circle of friends.

He thought to himself,
"I'm enjoying."

❧

In time, the adolescent became a young adult,
and prided himself on the things he did.

He thought to himself,
"I'm enjoying."

❧

In time, the young adult became an adult,
and prided himself on what he acquired in life.

He thought to himself,
"I'm enjoying."

❧

Then in time, the adult became an old man
who sat in the sun
and was nurtured by its warmth,
whose heart leaped at the dancing of a breeze,
and smiled warmly

at the dance of young lovers,
who laughed at the play of life,
and wept at every act of human kindness.

He thought to himself,
"I'm enjoying."

ೋೋ

He knew, now,
what his grandfather meant.

46

The Passing of the Torch

There lived a woman in the village of Tashkar
who all agreed was a most loving mother.

Whether at the market or in the temple,
or walking the village streets,
all took notice at how attentive she was
to her gentle and loving daughter.

"How sweet she is to her beloved child,"
a villager would say.

"There's no finer mother,"
would reply another.

But in the shelter of their home,
the mother would often say
to her young and loving daughter,

"You'll never amount to much."

And the little girl, ever obedient,
never did.

And in the shelter of their home,
the mother would often say
to her young and loving daughter,

"You're such an ugly little thing!
No worthy man will marry you!"

And the little girl, ever obedient,
married a brutish man.

And in the shelter of their home,
the mother would often say
to her young and loving daughter,

"I've never known happiness, nor shall you!"

And the little girl, ever obedient,
never did.

And in the shelter of their home,
the mother would often say
to her young and loving daughter,

"When you have children, you will see
what a disappointment they will be!"

And the little girl, ever obedient,
found this to be true.

When the child grew to womanhood,
and had a daughter of her own,
she, too, was said to be a most loving mother.

And whether at the market or in the temple,
or walking the village streets,
all took notice at how attentive she was
to her gentle and loving daughter.

"How sweet she is to her beloved child,"
a villager would say.

"There's no finer mother,"
would reply another.

But in the shelter of their home,
she would often say
to her young and loving daughter,

"You'll never amount to much."

And the little girl, ever obedient,
never did.

And like her mother, and her mother's mother,
and all that went before,
she was ever obedient.

47

The Poet's Skill at Fishing

A poet sat fishing on the bank of a pond.

After a time, a friend came along
and sat beside him;
sullen and dejected.

"What troubles you, my friend?"
asked the poet.
"You look so unhappy.
Here try some fishing.
That should cheer you up."

"Thank you," replied the friend.
"I'm not in the mood.

I've been struggling for weeks to create,
but nothing comes to me.
I've no inspiration. I'm a waterless well,
dried up and o' so barren."

"Be patient, my friend,"
said the poet, reassuringly.

"In time, ideas will begin to flow,
and you'll be creating happily once again."

"But it's been so long,"
the friend lamented.
What if nothing comes?

I've struggled, and tried,
and struggled again, but nothing inspires
or tickles my imagination.

You, on the other hand,
are always inspired.
What is your secret?"

The poet thought for a moment
then replied,

"Fishing."

The friend sat quiet,
a look of disbelief on his face.

"Yes, indeed," continued the poet,
"be the fisher of ideas!

You see, my friend, creating, like fishing,
requires patience and the utmost calm.

You cannot catch the fish;
the fish catches you.
You cannot catch an idea;
an idea catches you.

Be patient, and be calm.

Surround yourself in the beauty all about you
and let its enchantment work its creative magic.

Just be patient and receive it.

When the time is right, ideas will bite;
a nibble here, a nibble there.

Creativity will take your bait, my friend,
and soon you'll be hauling in
a boatload of ideas.

And, as all good fishermen know,
there'll be the good days and the bad ones;
again, be patient and be calm.

Yes, my friend, the secret to creating
is to be a fisherman of ideas,
just taking it as it comes."

Just then, he felt a pull upon his line
and soon, he had himself a wondrous fish.

He smiled gleefully, thanked the fish,
and threw it back into the water.

"Oh, and by the way,
don't forget to return to the pond
all that you have caught."

ഇൻ

The friend sat quietly,
eyes closed in silent introspection.

Soon ideas swam around his mind
and nibbled at his brain.

ഇൻ

Now that his friend was not looking,
the poet reached inside a bag he'd placed
beside a log
and tossed a handful of bait
into the awaiting pond.

He chuckled to himself
and whispered,

"And it doesn't hurt to seed the water,
either."

ഇൻ

He felt a tug at the end of his line.

A fish had taken his bait.

48

Rathgar Gets His Name

Great excitement filled the land,
for the Great Festival was soon approaching.
But those who now had come of age
were particularly excited,
for soon, they would get their name.

A teacher sat among the young
and explained to them,
The Tradition of the Naming.

"Each year, on the last night of
the Great Festival,
the young men and women
who reach the age of naming
enter, one by one, the Great Circle
and stand before the Wise Ones.

And the Wise Ones,
in their infinite wisdom,
would impart to each their name.

The first name is
the name given by your parents.

The second name is
the name that best describes your nature.

And the third name is
the name of your work among the people.

I am named,
Luthgar, Night Seer,
Teacher of the Children.

'Luthgar' is the name given by my parents.

'Night Seer' describes my nature to see
truths others do not see.

'Teacher of the Children'
is my work among the people.

The Wise Ones
are never wrong in their naming,
for they see deeply into each heart and soul.
They know you better than you
know yourself."

The teacher told a story.

₼ↂ

"There was once a boy named Rathgar.
He was the son of a great and mighty warrior.

Rathgar was a strong and handsome youth,
and none in his village could match him.

He loved to walk about with his head held high,
and to impress the girls,
would challenge each boy he met
to fight him if he dared.

When Rathgar came to the age of naming,
he was so excited he could not contain himself.
He knew he would be named a Warrior
like his warrior line before him.

'Rathgar, Lion Heart, Warrior,'
he would boast,
'That will be my name!'

or maybe,

'Rathgar, Leopard Fang, Warrior,'

either one will do.

When the Great Festival arrived,
and the last night soon approached,
Rathgar became so unbearable
no one would go near him.

Then, my children, the night of nights arrived
with its sacred time of naming

All the people gathered around
the Great Circle

and watched proudly as the children,
now of age,
stepped forth, one by one, and stood before
the Wise Ones to be given their life's name.

'Sanara, Wind Walker, Dancer!'

'Laneel, Catcher of Light, Artist!'

'Danga, Soothing Waters, Healer!'

'Kazden, Deep Roots, Tiller of the Fields!'

The last to enter the Great Circle
was Rathgar.

He strutted proudly out and stood tall
and straight before the Wise Ones,
ready to be given his name.

Rathgar,
Tiny Peacock,
Keeper of the Chickens!"

49

The Counting of the Stars

They looked to the sky at night
and counted all the stars they could,
and all, but one, placed value
in the *Counting of the Stars*.

They would gather high upon the hills
to await the setting sun,
and with the arrival of the night
would begin the timeless ritual of the
Counting of the Stars.

So important was the *Counting*,
all children from an early age
were taught the art and science
of accurately counting stars.

So sacred was the *Counting*,
priests of the Holy Temple
would remind the people always,
that Heaven awaits those
who count the most
in a life of counting stars.

୪ଓ

While all were busy counting stars,
one solitary woman looked up
and gazed, and dreamed, and wondered.

Her joy was simply in the watching,
and in a bright blue star.

She would gaze at this star in rapture,
as it touched her soul so deeply,
and she talked to it, and it to her,
of mystery, and of magic.

Her heart would dance within its light,
and her imagination wandered
to far off worlds, and far off times,
to her far off home among the stars.

The others did not love this star.
To them, it was just a number.

And they did not dream,
and did not wonder;
too busy were they in counting.

୪ଓ

She saw the sky and loved it,
and she knew it loved her, too.

But the others did not see the sky
for the
Counting of the Stars.

50

The Way of the Dreamer

In a land beyond the mist,
in a time when time was new,
a young boy dreamed.

He always dreamed,
much to the dismay of his elders.

While his classmates studied hard
the daily teachings,
the young boy gazed at the passing clouds
and saw in their shaping
wondrous beasts and fowl.

While in the fields with his father,
he would sit listlessly dreaming
of enchanted things
while his father tended to the growing.

At night, as he lay in his bed,
he would stare out his window

at the twinkling stars
and would dream of better worlds
and magic.

"He is a lazy boy,"
said the people of the village.
"He is an idle dreamer."
"He will not amount to much, I'm afraid."

"What will become of him?"
his loving parents lamented.
"What can we do?
Oh, what can we do?"

Each night, they prayed to Divine Mother
for guidance.

It was the *Autumn Time of Gathering;*
that time of year when the people gathered
to celebrate, to dance,
to talk of the year's harvest,
to work their many magics of together.

It was at this festival of gathering
that the strange man appeared
before his parents
as they sat conversing outside their tent;
the boy off somewhere dreaming.

"This is the time of Calling,"
spoke the strange man
in a soft and dreamy voice.

"I call your son to come with me
that he may learn the *Way of the Dreamer*."

In this time before time,
in this land now long forgotten,
such 'Callings' were known to happen
to a select few;
especially during times of festival.

The boy's parents knew that to be 'Called'
was the greatest of honors.

So, with heavy hearts,
they reluctantly agreed.

The following day,
with tearful farewells expressed,
the boy followed the stranger into the
Forbidden Land
to the secret City of Dreamers.

For eighty years, the boy learned the
Way of the Dreamer
til the day came when he,
now an old man,
was proclaimed by the Ancients of the city,
a 'Dreamer.'

He returned to the land of his birth
and spent a hundred years in a sacred garden
dreaming, and working his dreaming magic.

Every now and then,
a fortunate soul would find the way
to the sacred garden
to ask this Ancient One to dream
a dream into happening;
such was the magic of Dreamers.

ജ്ഞര

One day,
a farmer approached the Dreamer.

The Dreamer,
speaking in a soft dreamy voice, asked,
"What is the dream you seek?"

The farmer replied,
"Drought has stricken my field,
O' Great One.
Will you dream rain
to save my thirsting crops?"

The Dreamer asked,
"Tell me, dear one,
who is the author of all you behold?"

The farmer, hesitating not, replied,
"Why, you are, O' Great One!
You are the author of all I behold!"

The Dreamer, and the sacred garden,
faded away.

The farmer, confused,
found himself sitting alone in a field.

꽃

One day,
a father approached the Dreamer.

The Dreamer,
speaking in a soft dreamy voice, asked,
"What is the dream you seek?"

The father replied,
"My son is getting married, O' Great One.
Will you dream of a happy and abundant life
for my son and his wife to be?"

The Dreamer asked,
"Tell me, dear one,
who is the author of all you behold?"

The father thought for a moment then replied,
"Divine Mother is the creator of all I behold.
It is she who authors my life."

The Dreamer, and the sacred garden,
faded away.

The father, confused,
found himself sitting alone in a wood.

꽃

One day,
a mother with her dying child in her arms,
approached the Dreamer.

The Dreamer
spoke in a soft dreamy voice,
"What is the dream you seek?"

The crying mother replied,
"My child is dying of an incurable illness,
O' Great One,
I ask for a dream to save her."

The Dreamer asked,
"Tell me, dear one,
who is the author of all you behold?"

The mother thought long and deep.

"In truth, I am O' Great One.

Each of us authors all we behold;
we either create or allow it.
It was I who dreamt of you?"

The Dreamer smiled, closed his eyes,
and dreamt a dream of healing.

‼

In three days, the child was well enough
to run with her friends,
sing happy songs to her mother,
and dream the dreams of children.

ॐ

In a land beyond the mist,
in a time before time was new,
in a world now long forgotten,
such was the
Way of the Dreamer.

ॐ

Dearly beloved,
who is the author of all you behold,
and the author of this story?

51

The Laughing Fool of Binduvan

There lived high in the foothills
of the Kailesh Mountains,
in the tiny village of Binduvan,
a gentle man who laughed.

He laughed while he was awake,
and smiled while he was asleep,
and not one in the village of Binduvan
could recall a time
when he was not laughing or smiling.

He laughed so much,
the villagers thought him a fool.

One day,
two youths made a wager among themselves
to see who would be the first
to make the old fool cry.

While walking along a road,
on a dreary sunless day,
the two youths came upon the fool
sitting beneath a tree, giggling to himself.

"Come, my friend,"
said the first youth to the fool,
"We have something you must see.
You'll find it most amusing."

The youths took the fool to a nearby road
where lay a dead cat,
squashed by a passing cart.

The fool, in awe, exclaimed,
"Oh, look at its teeth!
How shiny white they are!"

Then he laughed with genuine delight.

The youths were much perplexed.

The second youth then said
to the delighted fool,
"Come, my friend,
we've something else to show you;
you'll find it most amusing."

The youths took the fool to a place
where a poor man, bowl in hand,
sat begging.

The fool, with glee, exclaimed,
"Oh, how industrious is that poor man!
And look how polite he is!"

Then he laughed with genuine delight.

The youths were much perplexed.

ৰ৹ঞ

Just then,
a busy merchant ran by on his way to work.
He fell and landed hard upon the ground,
breaking his leg in two.

The fool, in amazement, exclaimed,
"Oh, what a fortunate man!
Now he has time to enjoy
the magnificent beauty of nature!"

Then he laughed with genuine delight.

The youths, much perplexed,
walked away dejected.

ৰ৹ঞ

One afternoon,
while walking along a river path,
the fool noticed a woman taking time to stop
to attend to an old man
who lay dying by the river's edge.

She reached over and took the old man
in her arms and,

while gently cradling him,
sang him a sweet and tender song.

The old man passed peacefully away.

The fool wept sweet and tender tears
at such an act of human kindness.

52

The Thousand Coats of Suma Ti

Suma Ti wore a thousand coats;
some with bright and splendid colors,
some quite dark and faded,
others somewhere in between.

And when a coat became worn and tattered,
Suma Ti exchanged it for another.

෫෮

Suma Ti wore the coat of a warrior.
He fought many heroic battles
with courage and conviction
and took the lives of many.

And all the while, the Weaver Woman
gathered certain threads.

And when the coat became worn and tattered,
Suma Ti would exchange it for another.

ᥬ᭡꒱

Suma Ti wore the coat of a mother.
She gave birth to many children
and loved and nurtured all.

And all the while, the Weaver Woman
gathered certain threads.

And when the coat became worn and tattered,
Suma Ti would exchange it for another.

ᥬ᭡꒱

Suma Ti wore the coat of a thief.
He stole the dreams and hopes of others
and plundered precious memories.

And all the while, the Weaver Woman
gathered certain threads.

And when the coat became worn and tattered,
Suma Ti would exchange it for another.

ᥬ᭡꒱

Suma Ti wore the coat of a sailor.
He adventured the seas in all directions
and harbored in many exotic ports.

And all the while, the Weaver Woman
gathered certain threads.

And when the coat became worn and tattered,
Suma Ti would exchange it for another.

ॐ

Suma Ti wore the coat of a teacher.
She quenched the thirst for knowledge
in many inquisitive minds.

And all the while, the Weaver Woman
gathered certain threads.

And when the coat became worn and tattered,
Suma Ti would exchange it for another.

ॐ

Suma Ti wore the coat of a murderer.
He killed, and maimed, and made many suffer
without conscience or remorse.

And all the while, the Weaver Woman
gathered certain threads.

And when the coat became worn and tattered,
Suma Ti would exchange it for another.

ॐ

Suma Ti wore the coat of a holy woman.
She filled the hearts of all who knew her
with the sweetness of her love.

And all the while, the Weaver Woman
gathered certain threads.

And when the coat became worn and tattered,
Suma Ti would exchange it for another.

Suma Ti wore the coat of a healer.
She mended broken bones
as well as broken hearts.

And all the while, the Weaver Woman
gathered certain threads.

And when the coat became worn and tattered,
Suma Ti would exchange it for another.

When Suma Ti discarded the last coat,
and there were no more to be worn,
the Weaver Woman gathered
all the precious threads,
of all the thousand coats,
and weaved Suma Ti a cloak.

She spun a cloak of luminous light,
dazzling, bright, and wondrous,
and wrapped it gently around the shoulders
of the naked Suma Ti.

Then, Suma Ti, and the Weaver's Coat,
blended as one pure light.

And if you will, on a cloudless night,
look up to the eternal sky,
among the billions of brilliant stars,
look for Suma Ti.

53

In the Valley of
the Singing Stones

In a land long forgotten,
in a time before time was new,
there was a most magnificent place
where crystals sang
and Ancient Ones danced.

To the high mountains near the
northern coast,
to a hidden valley ringed by walls of stone,
a few would journey in hopes of finding the
Healing of the Singing Stones.

Neela was among the few
who sought this kind of healing.
Her illness was getting more severe
with each passing of the sun,
and she feared she was soon to die.

So Neela, gathering her remaining strength,
journeyed to the high mountains
near the northern coast,
to a hidden valley ringed by walls of stone,
in search of this healing place.

There were no trails or maps,
to mark this secret valley;
only the heart could guide you there,
and Neela's heart was strong indeed,
so, too, her unwavering hope.

Many weeks had passed,
and the journey was long and hard,
but Neela's heart would find the way to the
Valley of the Sing Stones.

৺

An Ancient Crone greeted her there.

৺

This old one laid Neela gently
upon a bed of leaves
within a ring of crystals
standing fifteen feet, or more.

Then the Crone began to dance,
slowly at first,
but in time, picked up the pace
till wildly she danced about
tapping crystals with her staff.

From each crystal came a beautiful sound,
and from each a beam of light.
Each crystal had its own clear tone,
each crystal its own pure light.

The beams ascended to the sky
and converged at a single point.
The sounds then lifted above that point
and became a silent tone.

All this above Neela,
who lay quiet upon the ground.

Then from that single point of light,
a laser beam descended,
and through that laser beam of light,
the silent tone flowed down.
Both entered into Neela,
who lay quiet upon the ground.

ॐ

Filled with light and sound,
the magic worked its magic,
and Neela felt her illness melt,
and her energy returning.

ॐ

Neela, now healed, thanked the Crone,
as well the Standing Stones,
and returned to her village once again
to live her healed life.

In a land long forgotten,
in a time before time was new,
there was a most magnificent place
where crystals sang,
and Ancient Ones danced.

54

Just Imagine

The Master sat with his disciples and spoke on
The Manifestation of One's Desires.

He spoke on and on
and all were enthralled and enraptured.

A woman in the back stood up
and gushed with delight.

"O' beloved Master, how happy I am!
My life overflows with lightness and joy!
I just can't imagine!"

The Master laughed and replied,
"But you did."

A year went by.

This time the Master spoke of
The Power of One's Belief.

Once again, the woman stood up
and gushed with delight.

"O' beloved Master, I have such good fortune!
My life overflows with much success
and achievement!
I just can't believe it!"

The Master laughed and replied,
"But you did."

&

Another year went by.

This time the Master spoke on the theme
We Create Our Own Reality.

Again, the woman stood up
and gushed with delight.

"O' beloved Master, I can't express
how loved I feel!
My life overflows with Divine Mother's love!
I just can't believe it! I just can't imagine!"

The Master laughed and replied,
"You did. You did."

&

Another year went by.

This time the Master spoke of
The Power of One's Imagination.

Again, the woman stood up
and gushed with delight.

"O' beloved Master, how beautiful life is!
My life is so rich and magical and full!
I just can't imagine!"

The Master laughed and replied,
"But you did."

It was many years before the woman
finally came to understand
her Master's strange reply;
can you believe that?

Just imagine!

55

A Marriage Made in Heaven

There lived a man who always found the bad
whenever times were good,
and always found the worse
whenever times were bad.

He'd always say how bleak things were,
since he had nothing else to say,
and never let himself be happy
out of fear it would go away.

Whenever someone said to him,
"My, how well you look!"
He'd shake his head and then reply,
"But eventually, I'll die."

And whenever someone said to him,
"Isn't it a beautiful day?"
He'd shake his head and then reply,
"It's going to rain tomorrow."

And whenever he achieved success
in anything he did,
people would congratulate him,
He'd shake his head and then reply,
"Ah' just luck. It'll never last."

And it never did.

ೞಣ

One day, while attending a festival,
which he thought was dull and boring,
he met a woman who attracted him,
and soon, they started talking.

ೞಣ

"What beautiful hair you have;
so black, and oh so wavy!"
The woman said to him.

He shook his head
and replied to her,
"Oh, it'll turn course and grey someday,
or probably just fall out."

"And what beautiful hands you have!"
She sweetly said to him.

He shook his head once more
and replied,
"Oh, I'll probably lose them
in a tragic accident."

ഏരു

Then he sweetly said to her,
"What beautiful skin you have!"

She shook her head
and then replied,
"Oh, it'll soon grow old and wrinkly."

"And what a beautiful smile you have!"
He sweetly said to her.

She shook her head once more
and said,
"Oh, it's okay for now,
but when I get old,
and my teeth fall out,
say that to me then."

ഏരു

They fell in love immediately,
and soon after that, they married,
and everyone who knew them well
say, to this very day,
"It was a marriage made in heaven."

56

The Eternal Companion

The two were inseparable;
this man and his dog.

They were always by each other's side
in the daytime and at night,
and the love he had
for his faithful companion
was a love that knew no bounds,
save one.

He believed his friend,
a form.

Throughout the day, both dog and man,
lived their lives together,
and through the night slept side by side;
two souls becoming one.

They'd frolic in the open fields,
or lie in the sheltering wood

listening to the talk of trees
as the wind passed through the branches.

Yes, he loved his dog
with a love that knew no bounds,
save one.

He believed his friend,
a form.

୫୦୬

But the day came, as such a day must do,
when the dog, the man's beloved friend,
let go of its mortal form.

୫୦୬

The man wept for days on end
from the pain of unbearable loss.
It's a pain that all in life must feel
when we believe that love is lost.
And though it will hurt much less in time,
it never goes away.

୫୦୬

The man believed himself alone,
though in truth he never was,
for his friend was always by his side,
though not in the form he knew.

Sadly, the man did not know this.
How could he?

He believed his friend
a form.

හඬ

Now, when he slept in the still of the night,
he believed he slept alone,
though his faithful friend lay by his side;
two souls still ever one.

Sadly, he did not know this.
How could he?

He believed his friend,
a form.

හඬ

Now, when the man walked through the field,
only bittersweet memories walked with him.

Sadly, he did not sense his friend
frolicking by his side.
How could he?

He believed his friend,
a form.

හඬ

Now, when he laid in the sheltering wood,
he heard only the mournful rustling of leaves.

Sadly, he did not hear his friend
whispering in the breeze,

"I love you, my friend! I always will!"
"I love you, my friend! I always will!"

And he whispered this to him always.
But how could he hear him?

He believed his friend,
a form.

Now, he faced his life alone,
or so he now believed.

Sadly, he did not sense his friend,
guiding him along.
How could he?

He believed his friend,
a form.

But, the day came, as such a day must do,
when the man let go of his mortal form.

On the other side,
waiting for him,
was his beloved loyal friend.

Now when they run and play and love,
it's far more real than it ever was before,
in this life beyond a form.

57

Manju Among the Saints

Manju traveled to the Valley of the Saints
to sit at the feet of the Holy Ones.

She sat at the feet of the four most enlightened
to hear them talk of the Divine.

"My disciples are like grains of sand
upon the desert;
too many to give a number,"
said the first.

"I speak to God always,"
said the second.
"He talks to me of the Divine."

"The miracles I perform are legendary,"
said the third.
"People gather from far and wide to behold
such wondrous workings."

The fourth just sat and giggled.

He giggled, and giggled,
and giggled some more,
oblivious to all around him.

଼ଠୡ

"I've composed many Sacred Texts,"
said the first.
"They're studied by all who seek the truth."

"I am bliss! I am light!"
gushed the second.
"I am Unbounded Oneness!"

"My portrait hangs in holy temples,"
said the third.
"and mothers give their young my name."

The fourth just sat and giggled.

He giggled, and giggled,
and giggled some more,
oblivious to all around him.

଼ଠୡ

Manju stood, passed gas,
then sat in the cool of a spreading tree
where there was less noise.

58

The Selfishly Generous Woman

She was such a wonderfully generous woman
who gave, and gave, and gave.

She always made a special point
of giving special little gifts
on all those special little occasions
to all her special family,
and all her special friends.

She'd always walk that extra mile
when the festivals arrived
to make all around her happy,
and their celebrations bright.

She'd fuss, and bother, and take the time
to see that all were catered to,
and all were having fun.

But, heaven help those who gave to her,
for she'd always break their hearts.

ഇരുന്

When someone gave a gift to her,
she'd always gush and spout,
"Oh, why did you go to so much trouble?
I really don't deserve this!"

"No, please, no! You shouldn't have!
I really can't accept it!"

Then she'd either give it back,
or reluctantly accept it,
or she'd purchase something twice the price
and gift it to the giver.

ഇരുന്

She hated herself inside
and not worthy of the love of others.
And it made her mad when others gave
their precious love to her.

For you see,
she'd much rather be right about herself,
than ever to be loved.

She was too selfish to realize
the harm she caused to others
by turning away their love.

It was her selfishness
that bruised the hearts
of all who cared for her.

By selfishly not accepting love,
we keep others from the giving,
for people need to express their hearts.
It's essential to their loving.

How can people practice giving
if no one's there receiving?

In time, her friends and family
drifted emotionally away.

In time, she felt alone
and valueless and unloved,
which is what she always believed
about herself.

But, then again,
she'd rather be right than loved.

59

The Master's Perfect Imperfection

There lived a wise and enlightened Master
who experienced many misfortunes,
much to the confusion of his faithful disciples.

"O' Master!" they'd ask,
"How can a man of your enlightenment
experience such misfortune?"

The Master would simply laugh and say,

"Such is life,"
and chuckle merrily to himself.

ॐ

When the enlightened Master's house
burned down,
much to the confusion of his faithful disciples,
they asked him,

"O' Perfect One,
how can life be so imperfect
for a perfect one like you?"

"But, I now live in a better house,"
replied the Master.
"one more suited to my liking.

Such is life!"

ഇരു

When the enlightened Master became
gravely ill,
much to the confusion of his faithful disciples,
they asked him,

"O' Illumined Master,
how can such a bad thing happen
to a saint at one with God?"

"I needed to slow down,"
replied the Master.
"and I much enjoyed the rest.

Such is life!"

ഇരു

When the enlightened Master's
potato garden perished,
much to the confusion of his faithful disciples,
they asked him,

"O' Wise and Beloved Master,
how can such a bad thing happen
to one so good as you?"

"Did I not desire tomatoes?"
replied the Master.
"Now they grow in my garden;
so large and very tasty.

Such is life!"

൞൞

"Life's a roll of the dice,"
the Master would often say,

"The enlightened know this to be true.
So, they simply load the dice."

൞൞

One day,
while riding in his wagon
on the way to preside at a sacred festival,
his driver hit a bump and broke a wheel in two.

The Master smiled,
for it happened in front of a wheel makers shop.

൞൞

And the sacred festival?
It started late anyway.

"Such is life!"

60

King or Seeker

He was born the eldest of thirty sons,
and the most beloved of his father,
King Darantha.

Handsome and brave,
all the maidens of all the lands far and wide
were his for the claiming.

He was learned in all the sciences,
and excelled in all the arts,
and well versed was he in the teachings
of the holy Sacred Texts.

Yes, he was a prince of great fortune
and splendid gifts
and a day would come when all he beheld
would pass to him upon the death
of the great king, Darantha.

But, for all his vast fortune and blessed gifts,
his soul yearned and could not find peace;
for his was the soul of a seeker.

He was destined to the search

৪৩

One day, he made a fateful decision.

Ignoring the protestations of the King
and High Priests,
and ignoring the beseechings
of his beloved family,
he left the palace
in search of an enlightened master,
whose wisdom and presence
would quench his thirsting soul.

৪৩

For many years he traveled the corners
of the earth
searching for his master.
He met many great saints along the way,
but none could satisfy his thirst.

It was in the blessed form
of the great sage, Gundavama,
that his thirsting soul would find refreshment,
and it was in the loving heart
of this illumined master,
that he, at last, found home.

He stayed with Gundavama for many years,
basking in his light and wisdom,
and he grew in knowledge and understanding
of the sacred and divine.

And it was through the love
of his master, Gundavama,
that he awakened his love for Her:
The blessed Mother Divine.

৺৶

His passion was to sit beneath his favorite tree
on the bank of a forest river,
listening to her voice in all the forest sounds:
The Voice of Mother Divine.

His passion was to sit beneath his favorite tree
on the bank of a forest river,
beholding her face in everything,
and everyone:
The Face of Mother Divine.

He was truly happy, completely free,
and totally at peace.

৺৶

One day,
his brothers arrived at the forest cave
of the great sage Gundavama
in search of their eldest brother.

When they saw him, they fell to the ground
and cried out with joy.

"Oh, blessed are we to gaze upon you,
beloved brother!"
"We've journeyed long to find you.

We bring sad news, however."

They wept bitterly.

"Our beloved king and father, Darantha,
has left his mortal form
and is now in boundless bliss.

You, dear brother, are now our king.

We come to bring you back
to a land and people much in need of your
love and able guidance."

ॐ

Pained was he to hear this news,
and greatly troubled by it,
for he knew not what to do.

Should he go back with his brothers
and fulfill the obligations of his birth?
His beloved people need him.

Or should he remain with his beloved Master,
his beloved forest,
and his beloved Mother Divine?

Should he answer the call of his duty?
or
Answer the call of his heart?

ॐ

Gundavama spoke not a word.
The decision must be his,
and his alone.

ᔕᔡ

Beneath the full moon, in the sill of night,
he struggled much over what to do.

By the dawn of the next day,
he made his fateful decision.

He returned with his brothers,
and became a king.

ᔕᔡ

He ruled wisely, and with justice,
and the people were happy,
and the love they felt for him had no bounds.

Indeed,
the land and people were truly blessed.
And for the remainder of his life,
the kingdom he ruled
grew and prospered.

But, he did not.

ᔕᔡ

His spirit died that fateful night,
and his soul wept for what was lost.

He became a shadow,
moving ghost-like through his life;
unhappy and in pain.

In time, he died of a broken heart.

Should he have remained a seeker?
Did he choose rightly to be a king?

It wasn't until many lifetimes
that he came to realize,
he could have had them both.

61

Where the Two Worlds Meet

In a meadow, two trees grow,
between them, an invisible door;
on one side, the Realm of Faerie,
on the other, the Realm of Man.

She was a daughter of the Fae,
he a son of Human,
and although their worlds divided,
their souls entwined as one.

He met her in the Faerie Realm
while collecting crystals in a stream.
At first, he thought her like himself;
she knew he was a Human.

They walked awhile and laughed,
she sang for him a fairy song,
he placed a crystal in her hand,
lovers they became.

For years they traveled together
between the shimmering Realm of Fae,
and the denser Realm of Man,
and always by each other's side.

He worked his human magic,
she, the fefa of her race,
and together, they healed injured things
and woke the sleeping crystals.

Mostly they worked together
for the healing of the earth,
for Human and Faerie magic
make a powerful combination.

Although in time he died,
and she lived on for countless years,
their souls remained entwined,
not bound by fleeting time.

ഇരു

Four hundred years have come and gone,
and a man of the race of Human
stands in a meadow before two trees,
on the other side, a daughter of the Fae.

They stand before an invisible door
ready to resume their love,
and unite once more
the shimmering Realm of Fae
with the denser Realm of Man.

They'll walk awhile and laugh,
she'll sing for him a fairy song,
he'll place a crystal in her hand,
and lovers they'll become.

The earth needs lovers such as these,
and the workings of their magics,
for there's much healing to be done
and crystals to be awakened.

In a meadow, two trees grow,
between them, an invisible door;
on one side, the Realm of Faerie,
on the other, the Realm of Man.

62

My Life Has Never Been So Bad

There lived a woman who always complained
whenever she found herself buffeted
by the raging storms of change and crisis.

"My life has never been so bad!"
she was often heard to say;
then she'd curse herself for failing
at the living of her life.

And when the storm was over,
and the crisis come and gone,
she'd smile to all her friends and say,
"Oh, how my life is better now
then it's ever been before!"

ॐ

Year after year, crisis after crisis,
it would always be the same.
"My life has never been so bad,"

then she'd curse herself for failing
at the living of her life.

And when the drama ended,
she'd smile to her friends and say,
"Oh, how my life is better now
then it's ever been before!"

સેલ્

Eventually, she took notice
of her predictably strange behavior,
and withdrew into herself
to discover why she did it.

"If, out of every crisis,
my life has turned the better,
then how can crises be so bad,
and I, in life, a failure?"

She came to realize that a crisis
is a normal part of living
and even quite essential
on our path to becoming more.

It's the place we find ourselves
when the old of us is gone,
and a place we find ourselves
when the new has yet to come.

She realized that a crisis
is not a sign of failure,
or that we're bad or wrong,

but an essential part of life's transition
to a better us ahead.

ജന

Now, when she finds herself in crisis,
it's no longer a raging storm,
but merely a summer drizzle
on her path to becoming more.

"My life has never been so good,"
she now would always say,
and in time, she came to realize
it was always, in truth, that way.

63

Mother Seagull
and the Ocean

While walking along the beach,
a teacher said to his disciple,
"Let's stop a while;
I have a tale I wish to tell."

They sat together upon the sand,
and the teacher told his story.

"Mother Seagull loved her children
and would happily play with them
by the edge of the mighty ocean.

Ocean, watching their loving play,
became jealous and said to himself,
'I desire Mother Seagull's children,
for I, too, wish to dance and sing.'

So, with a mighty wave,
he swept up the tiny chicks
and carried them out to sea.

Mother Seagull, horrified,
begged and pleaded for their return,

'Please! Please, great Ocean!
Please return my precious children!'

Ocean just laughed his roaring laugh
and held tightly to the trembling chicks.

Mother Seagull then said to Ocean,
'If you will not return my children,
I'll take this sand within my beak
and throw it upon your waves,
and on and on I'll throw the sand
until you are no more.'

Ocean just laughed his roaring laugh
and held tightly to the trembling chicks.

'O' Mother Seagull, you are but a little thing
compared to the might of me.

No bigger are you then a speck of sand
by the edge of the endless sea.
Do what you will, O' little bird,
I'll not return your chicks.'

Mother Seagull filled her beak with sand,
then threw them upon the waves.
Over and over, again and again,

she tossed the tiny grains of sand
upon the endless sea.

ॐ

Eagle,
the Lord of Birds,
observing Mother Seagull's plight,
and admiring her tenacity,
ordered all the birds of the sky
to come and give her help.

And soon they too were tossing sand
upon the endless sea.

ॐ

Lion,
the Lord of Beasts,
observing Mother Seagull's plight,
and admiring her tenacity,
ordered all the beasts of the earth
to come and give her help.

And soon they too were pushing sand
upon the endless sea.

ॐ

Sun,
watching in amazement as the birds
and beasts of the earth gathered as one
to help the little seagull,
joined in as well.

He cast his heat upon the water
turning it to steam.

Wind,
taking pity on Mother Seagull,
blew her mighty breath upon the sand
sending it flying out to sea.

Earth,
the Most Compassionate,
joined as well.

She shook, and shook,
and shook some more
sending mountains crashing
down upon the shrinking waves.

Ocean became very frightened,
for he was getting smaller and smaller
and would soon be no bigger than a pond.

In desperation,
he begged Mother Seagull,
'Stop, Mother Seagull!
Please stop!
I'll give you back your children!'

And with a tiny wave,
for he was now very small, indeed,
returned the chicks to their awaiting,
and very tired, mother.

ॐ

To this day,
Ocean will never do anything
to upset Mother Seagull.”

ॐ

“So,” said the teacher to the disciple,
“What did you learn from this tale?”

The disciple thought for a moment,
then replied,

“Be faithful and tenacious
with the calling of your heart,
for in so doing,
all of Nature will come to your support,
even if you are a pain in the ass.”

ॐ

The teacher’s jaw dropped
as he stared in shock and horror
by the disciple’s choice of words.

“Well, ah… Well, ah…”
he stammered,
“Well, let’s get something to eat.”

64

The Man
Who Talked With Trees

There lived a man who was different.

The people of his village thought him odd
and somewhat of a fool,
and to his good fortune, he was.

He seldom did what others did;
it was simply not his way.

When the people prayed in the Holy Temple,
the man would sit in his beloved forest
and talk with his beloved trees.

When the people sought the counsel
of wise masters,
the man would go to his beloved forest
to seek the counsel of trees.

While the people quoted
the wisdom of others,
the man would sit in his beloved forest
absorbing the wisdom of trees.

ॐ

"Come, a great Master is among us!"
the people would tell him.
"Come hear him speak of universal truths!"

The man would politely nod, then go instead
to his beloved forest to learn universal truths
from the teachings of an oak.

ॐ

"Come, a great Master is among us!"
the people would tell him.
"Come, hear him speak of mystery,
and of magic!"

The man would politely nod, then go instead
to his beloved forest to learn true mystery,
and true magic,
from the teachings of a willow.

"Come, a great Master is among us!"
the people would tell him.
"Come, hear him speak of the sacred
and divine!"

The man would politely nod, then go instead
to his beloved forest to bathe

in the sacred and divine
from the teachings of a pine.

෩෬

In time, the man grew to become
a wise and holy master,
well known throughout the land.

He would travel from village to village
sharing all he learned
from his beloved trees.

෩෬

"Come, a great Master is among us!"
the people would shout,
and they gathered at his feet
and basked in his holy presence.

They memorized his teachings,
and quoted his every word,
but they did not understand him,
for they knew nothing of the trees.

65

Mukta and the Magic Purse

Mukta was a poor man.

He did not live in a stately mansion,
or ride in a gilded cart.
He had no servants or fine horses,
or any of the grand things
the noble folk possessed.

But, Mukta had all he ever wanted,
and all he would ever need
and, it should be noted,
he possessed a magic purse.

What was strange about this wondrous purse
was that it was always empty.

But, whenever Mukta reached
his hand within, and pulled it out,
within his palm were enough gold coins
to pay for what he needed.

ೞಿಲ್ಲ

One day, Mukta's greedy brother,
marveling at this splendid purse, exclaimed,
"Mukta, where did you get such a purse?"

"From a wandering holy man," Mukta replied.
"He gave it to me for doing him a kindness."

Mukta's greedy brother grew envious
and decided to steal the magic purse.

ೞಿಲ್ಲ

One day, while Mukta meditated
beneath a tall willow tree,
his brother stole the magic purse
and replaced it with another.

But when the greedy brother got home,
and put his hand within the purse,
he found it empty,
not a single coin within it.

Angry, the greedy brother raced back
to Mukta's house just in time to see Mukta
pulling out a handful of bright gold coins
from the other purse.

"What's this!" cried the greedy brother.
"How can you pull coins from that purse?
It's fake!"

223

"Oh, foolish brother," replied Mukta,
"did you think the magic was in the purse?"

He laughed, then said to his greatly
distressed brother,
"The magic is not in the purse, dear brother;
the magic is in me."

66

Sinji's One and Only Tale

Sinji was the most famous of storytellers,
beloved of the people of the tall trees,
and those of the enchanted harbors,
beloved of those who toiled
in the high mountains,
and those who worked the fertile fields
in the valleys far below.

Yes, Sinji was a beloved storyteller,
a masterful magician of wondrous magic,
and a teller of a single story,
his one and only tale.

When Sinji entered a village,
all the people would gather at night
around a roaring fire
and listen in silence as he spun
his one and only tale.

When Sinji left the village,
he left a place much different than before.
The village prospered,
and the lives of the people changed.

But there was something strange
about Sinji
and his one and only tale.

No one ever heard what Sinji said exactly,
and what was heard, in truth,
he really did not say.

His tale was woven in the mind
of each villager who heard it,
and in the flickering images,
the mind imagined,
in the dancing of the flames.

An old one may hear a story
of times long past
when the world was a better place,
while a merchant may hear a tale of riches
and the hunt for wealth and treasures.

A warrior may hear of battles
and legendary heroes,
while lovers may hear a romantic tale
of a love that lives forever.

A child may hear of the hidden folk,
and worlds of magic and enchantment,

while an adolescent may hear of kings
and queens,
and tales of great adventures.

ഔന

His tale was what you wanted it to be,
or needed it to be at the time,
and all who heard it grew and changed,
or they left it as a fantasy.

But, in time, change happened anyway,
even to those who thought it a fantasy.

There's great magic in imagination,
and there's magic in the telling.

ഔന

So, what was Sinji's one and only tale?

I have no idea;
I heard something different.

67

A Simple Tale of Hope

Two men,
while traveling on a high mountain road,
found themselves stranded
on a small ledge
extending over a valley
hundreds of feet below.

They could not move,
for they were trapped by a sudden
winter storm.

"We're doomed!
There's no hope for us!"
cried the first man.

"Don't give up hope, my friend."
replied the second, calmly.

"Hope brings with it miracles,
and as I see it,
we're much in need of
a miracle right now."

"But the storm is growing fierce,
and on this mountain
none have survived the rage
of a winter storm!"
wailed the first man.

"Calm yourself, my friend."
replied the second.
"Let me share with you a story,
and pray, it gives you hope.

ಬಲ

'A great flood swept the lower plains
crushing all the villages in its path
and taking with it countless lives.

Three women miraculously survived
the disaster by clinging tightly
to a floating log.

For many miles,
the three women held desperately to the log
despite being viciously pummeled
by the crashing water.

The first woman, tired and weak,
sighed helplessly,
'There's no hope for us!'
and loosened her grip on the log
and perished beneath the muddy waves.

'Do not give up hope!
cried the third woman.

229

'We'll survive
if we hold tightly to our hope.'

⁎

For many more miles,
the two remaining women
clung to the slippery log.

'I cannot hold on any longer!
There's no hope for us!'
wept the second woman,
and loosened her grip on the log
and disappeared beneath
the raging water.

A few seconds later,
the log floated around a bend
and landed safely on a dry bank.

The hopeful woman was safe at last."

⁎

"Be damned with your foolish story!"
shouted the first man. "Are you insane?
What does that story have to do
with our plight? Your tale is a fantasy!
We're in the real world now!
Hope will not save us here!"

The man became more upset,
and started angrily paced back and forth.

Suddenly, the ledge beneath his feet
broke from the weight of his pacing
sending him crashing to his death below.

A few seconds later, the storm broke,
and the weather grew calm.

The hopeful man walked down the mountain
to the valley below.

When he reached the safety of the valley,
the raging storm continued
on the mountain once again.

68

Coming Home

There lived an old woman who was loved.

All the people in her small village
spoke kindly of her
and felt blessed she lived among them.

She gave all she had to those less fortunate,
and tended compassionately
to the sick and dying.

She played games with the children,
and listened attentively
to the ramblings of the young.

She gave wise counsel to those in love,
and to those
still desperately searching.

And all who came to this old woman's door
were welcomed as her child.

And the people called her "Mother."

There also lived an old man who was
much despised.

All the people in his small village
felt unkindly toward him
and felt ashamed he lived among them.

He hated all and shunned their company,
preferring to be left alone.

He stole, and cheated, and lied,
and did all manner of
evil things,
for his heart was cold and bitter.

No one came to this old one's door,
for none were welcomed there.

And the people never spoke of him at all.

When the time came for both to pass,
Compassionate Death
appeared.

He took each one by the hand
and guided them lovingly
to the awaiting arms of God and Goddess.

The old woman,
overwhelmed by their infinite love,
wept.

God and Goddess spoke.

"Oh, dear beloved child,
it is we who are overwhelmed by your return;
no words can express our joy!"

The old man,
overwhelmed by their infinite love,
also wept.

God and Goddess spoke.

"Oh, dear beloved child,
it is we who are overwhelmed by your return;
no words can express our joy!"

"But, I lived an evil life,"
cried the old man.
"I do not deserve your love.
Why do you love me, so?"

God and Goddess spoke tenderly
to them both.

"We have no reason for loving you;
we love you for no reason at all.

Our love for you is always more
without it ever being less.

There's nothing you could ever do
that would make us love you more,
and nothing you could ever do
that would make us love you less.

We love no one more, and no one less,
and no one is loved the same.
And yes, my children, it is true,
we've always known your name.

Come home, dear ones, and rest awhile
before you journey back."

☙❧

"But why can't we stay with you,
forever in your embrace?"
the old woman asked.

"You could, but you have chosen not,"
was their reply to her.

"Out of love and out of grace,
all have made a choice.
To keep on growing is your grace;
making love much more, your choice."

☙❧

God and Goddess took the old woman,
and the old man in their loving arms

and carried them tenderly home.

If only for a while.

69

Sumitra and Her Friends

Although the only child of a farmer
and his wife,
Sumitra was never alone,
for she had many friends.

She would spend her days
with her beloved friends
exploring the forbidden forests,
and dancing freely among the wildflowers
in the wild enchanted meadows.

They taught her the language
of growing things,
and how to work the magic
of the crystals
they gathered in the streams.

They dreamed together beneath the trees
and chased the forest beasts.
They swam among the fishes of the ponds
and played hide and seek with the wind.

At night they taught her the names of stars
and told her their fairy stories,
and they'd listen in wonder
to the melodious sounds
of the creatures of the dark.

Although others could not see her friends,
they were clearly seen by her.

But, sadly, as time so often makes it,
Sumitra grew and drifted away,
and played less and less with unseen friends,
and more with human children.

In time,
she discovered the mystery of boys.

In time,
the pull of love.

In time,
she played no more with childhood friends
she could no longer see.

In time,
she entered the grown-up world.

In time,
she had a husband and two children.

In time,
she performed her grown-up duties
with its many obligations.

In time,
she forgot all childish things,
and forgot her childhood friends.

ॐ

But sadly, as time so often makes it,
Sumitra grew old and feeble.

With a body now bent and racked with pain,
and a husband passed, and children grown,
Sumitra lived alone,
her memories now her friends.

ॐ

And sadly, as time so often makes it,
Sumitra died alone and unhappy,
and sadly, in time, forgotten.

ॐ

Each spring, wildflowers grow upon her grave
in the shape of a crimson heart,
flowers lovingly tended
by her beloved unseen friends.

70

The Sweet Old Couple

He stares out the window;
she stares at her cup of tea.
They stopped talking a long time ago.
Perhaps they never did.

This is how their life is now.
Perhaps it was always so.

And the love they had,
or thought they had,
died a long time ago.

ഔଔ

"I know him like the back of my hand!"
she'd tell others with a dismissive sigh.
He would shake his head
and say nothing.

They stopped knowing one another
when they figured each other out.

And the love they had,
or thought they had,
died a long time ago.

೫೦೧೩

He remembers things he never did;
she remembers loves she never knew.
And together, they remember
the grand times,
those times that never were.

They do not touch each other anymore,
and cannot remember when last they did.
Now she touches only the cat,
and he, his wooden cane.

And the love they had,
or thought they had,
died a long time ago.

೫೦೧೩

Once they lived together
because that is what you did,
had children
because that's what was expected.

"Well, of course, they had children.
Who else would take care of them
in their later years?"

Now they stay together
because there's nowhere else to go,

and they can barely remember
the names
of their children anymore.

And the love they had,
or thought they had,
died a long time ago.

ಙಔ

Passersby smile when they see them sitting
side by side.

Young lovers hold each other close
and say, wistfully,

"Oh, honey, how sweet they are!"
"I hope our love remains that strong
when we become their age."

71

A Most
Unconventional Master

A disciple decided to be just like
his Master.

Since his Master always wore
a robe of white,
he too put on a robe of white.

The next day, the Master appeared
wearing the multi-colored robe
of a merchant.

The disciple was confused.

৵০৶

Since the Master's hair was long
and straight,
the disciple grew his hair long
and straight.

The next day, the Master appeared
with his hair cut and shaped
in the latest style.

The disciple was confused.

ஐஇ

Since every afternoon
the Master sat eyes closed
in deep silence,
every afternoon the disciple sat
eyes closed in deep silence.

But, then,
the Master no longer spent
his afternoons
sitting with eyes closed
in deep silence.
Instead, he spent his afternoons
dancing.

The disciple was confused.

ஐஇ

Since the Master dined on
white rice and mung dal,
so too, the disciple dined on
white rice and mung dal.

That is until the disciple noticed
his Master eating a bowl of rocks.

The disciple was confused.

ഇരുബ

The Master smiled mischievously,
then burped.

72

The Secret of Sima Sen

The people thought her a wise
and holy woman,
some even called her a Saint.

Not because she was versed
in the Sacred Texts,
she wasn't;
or because she had disciples,
she didn't;
or because she meditated
for hours every day,
she couldn't.

but because of her kindness
and the richness she brought to herself
and to all the people around her.

People would ask her,
"Sima Sen, what is the secret
that makes you so?

There must be some magic,
some mystery, some knowledge,
that allows you such grace,
such happiness, such kindness."

Sima Sen would smile and reply,
"I just listen and respond."

ॐ

Sima Sen wanted for nothing.
Although she was not wealthy,
she had all she ever needed,
and all she ever wanted.

Sima Sen was never ill,
though she never saw a healer,
or took the healing herbs.

Sima Sen was never without love,
though she never married,
or had children.

Sima Sen was never sad,
though she did not possess the things
that made others happy.

She was just, well, Sima Sen.

People would ask her,
"Sima Sen, what is the secret
that makes you so?"

"There must be some magic,
some mystery, some knowledge,
that allows you such an abundant
and bountiful life."

Sima Sen would smile and reply,
"I just listen and respond."

ഇരു

Sima Sen did one thing,
others would not do.
She'd ventured alone in the
Darkened Wood.

Being such a terrifying place,
filled with voices and apparitions,
people refused to enter that
dark and forbidden forest.

ഇരു

One day, a woman followed Sima Sen
into the Darkened Wood.

She hoped to discover a secret there
to be like Sima Sen.

ഇരു

Sima Sen entered a grove of trees
at the very heart of the forest
and sat beneath the ancient
Grandmother Tree.

Suddenly, there appeared before her
a group of people.

Some were very young,
others in their teens.
Some were in their adult years,
others very old.

All but a few looked like Sima Sen
throughout the stages of her life.

Some would get very angry at her,
and would shout and flail about,
Some would sit and quietly listen
to the speaking of her heart.

The children would sit by Sima's side
holding her very tight.
The elders stood behind her, smiling
with love and understanding,
and genuine delight.

And all the while, Sima Sen
sat patiently and listened,
and gave to each and every one
her complete and full attention.

When all was said that needed to be said,
and all was done that needed to be done,
the many Sima Sens, satisfied,
suddenly turned and vanished.

As Sima Sen stood up to leave,
the woman, confused, approached her.

"What just happened, Sima Sen?"
the woman asked.
"Who were those many people?
And why did they look so much
like you?"

Sima Sen replied,

"What you saw were my many selves,
some are less, and some are more.

When the lesser of me are feeling troubled,
they try to get my attention.
Whenever I'm unhappy, or in anger,
or feeling fear, or pain,
I know they call out to me.

So, I go to them and listen
and give my full attention,
and I always give my love.

Some of my selves are quite unpleasant;
some are much wiser than me,
but if you can love the least of you,
and heed the counsel of the more,
then, my friend, you'll love your life,
and grow to love you more.

The magic is just to listen,
and respond,
and to give them your full attention."

ജ

Sima Sen walked home feeling whole
and more at peace
for having listened and responded.

73

The Sweet Taste of Vindication

A poor boy lived in a small village
not many miles from here.

The people of the village
scoffed and chided
whenever they would see him,
and made his life a living hell;
so severely did they treat him.

The other children laughed at him
and made fun of his tattered clothes.
They stole what little food he had
and beat him till he cried.

As this poor boy walked
the streets alone,
people looked the other way,
not seeing his tearful eyes.

Sometimes he'd hear them say,
"Filthy little beast. He smells so bad!"

"Is there a boy beneath such dirt? "
"What a pitiful, useless child!"
"He'll never amount to much."

Then they whispered, and laughed,
and arrogantly walked away.

He swore to himself,
"One day, I'll prove them wrong!
They'll see! They'll see!"

෩෨

When he got older,
he left the village and traveled
to a great city.
There, he toiled and sacrificed
and endured much pain and hardship.

He worked, and learned,
and worked some more,
and all the while he swore,
"One day, I'll prove them wrong!
They'll see! They'll see!".

෩෨

He allowed no time for laughter
and allowed no time for play,
and, to him, love was just a
waste of time.

He knew the time would come someday
when his dream would be achieved,

a dream born of a wounded child,
a dream of vindication.

And, in time, that time did come

ॐ

He became a great and powerful man,
a man of wealth, of fame, of stature.

Yet, for all his fame and
accomplishments,
his hatred grew ever stronger.

Many admired him; few loved him,
but he didn't care.
He proved them wrong,
and that was all that mattered.

ॐ

Then one day, that 'one day' came.

He returned to the village
to show to everyone
how wrong they were about him,
and, of course, he came to gloat.

But, no one remembered him.

They did not remember his face,
or recognize his name.
They heard nothing of his wealth,
or fame,
or of his many accomplishments.

And, when they did, frankly,
they didn't care.

The boy,
now a man of great wealth and fame,
sat upon a rock and wept.

74

What Kamila Learned from a Chipmunk

Kamila did everything in moderation.
'Not too much, and not too little,'
was how she lived her life,
and
'Everything in its proper place,
and in its proper time.'

❦

She never did anything to excess,
for to do so would be indulgent,
and, in the eating of her life,
nibbled morsels at a time.

She never got excited,
and never got depressed,
and sailed through life on a sea of calm,
on a steady, even course.

❦

One day, while sitting in her garden,
she noticed a little chipmunk
scurrying busily about.

She watched in amazement as the little
chipmunk filled his tiny mouth
so wide with nuts
she thought he was going to burst.

Then, with cheeks puffed out,
he scrambled back into his hole
to store his precious catch.

Back and forth he scurried,
delighting in his frenzy.
One-minute puffing wide with nuts,
the next, back in his hole.

ಬಿಂ

She thought about her life,
and how unlike this little chipmunk
her boring life became.

She never puffed, and never scurried,
and never felt delight,
and never once had she ever plunged
down a darkened hole.

When anything exciting happened to her,
she never, with gusto, gobbled it up,
then race wildly about,
and never, like the chipmunk,

stored the treasured memories
of the gobbling and the catch.

Her life was a boring
'one nut at a time'
affair.

ॐ

One day, while having cake with friends,
she shouted out with great satisfaction,
"To hell with my diet, Agnes!
Please pass to me a second!"

She filled her cheeks wide with cake
and gobbled it all up, with
gusto and delight.

75

Galen's Glimpse of Hell

Galen was an evil man
who murdered, raped, and pillaged.

He took all, gave nothing, and did it all
without conscience or remorse.

He lived in hate and dined on rage,
and wallowed in every temporal sin.

Devoid of all compassion,
or the slightest bit of kindness,
Galen showed no trace of mercy
to the many that he harmed.

He did not feel love or sympathy,
or any lofty emotion,
and would not allow himself happiness,
or joy, or laughter,
as he thought such things a weakness.

So, when he died, it was no surprise
when he found himself walking down

a long corridor on his way to the
Gates of Hell.

ဆ၁ၶ

At the end of the darkened passage,
beside a blackened gate,
a fearsome sentinel cloaked in red
silently watched and waited.

When Galen approached
and stood before the Gate of Hell,
the silent sentinel, with a dourer look,
bellowed these words to him.

"Behold!
Beyond this blackened gate lies
the Hell that you have wrought!"

Galen looked beyond the gate,
and to his great surprise,
he saw the life he left behind
playing out before his eyes.

He stood in shock and silence
as he watched his life unfold,
and what he saw he hated.

As he relived each painful moment
of the life he left behind,
he shuttered and cried out,

"Oh, no! Oh, no!
How could I have been so blind?"

He fell upon the ground in shame,
and curled up like a newborn child.

For a man who never shed a tear,
he wept so loud, and cried so deep,
from a place in him long hidden.
He wept till he could cry no more,
then lay silent upon the floor.

"Life is Hell,"
spoke the guardian cloaked in red.
"but, it can also be your Heaven,
or somewhere in between.

God and Goddess gave each and all
a single wondrous gift,
the blessed gift of choice.

Your life becomes what you choose it be,
a heaven, or a hell,
or somewhere in between.

In your next life, my friend,
why not choose a little better?"

Galen took another life,
and this time made a better choice,
a choice somewhere in between,
for now.

76

Being Real

He meets his Higher Self
in a clearing in the wood
just as he does every night.

They talk together, laugh together,
cry together,
and, of course, love together.

They work as partners in the workings
of their magic,
in the casting of dreams and visions,
in the seeding of their hopes,
in the making of a map
for a world that's yet to be.

Sometimes they travel on adventures
to a bright blue star
where friends and teachers wait,
and memories of home.

Sometimes to the Imaginal Realm
where imagination imagines itself
and virgin futures await to be imagined.

Sometimes they journey to the
Realm of Fairie
to work their magic with the children of the
Tuartha de Danaan.

Then off to the Valley of the
Standing Stones,
or to that place beyond the mist
where the Mystic Mill still stands.

Or, he lies in this clearing in the wood
to be healed, replenished, and renewed,
by a nurturing Soul, and his loving
Higher Self.

And in this clearing in the wood,
he lifts his lesser parts of self,
and is raised by his parts more real.

And in the dark places of himself,
he seeks a spark of light.

And, of course, he dances
with God, Goddess, All That Is,
a graceful dance, a sensuous dance,
a dance of wild abandon.

And, he loves and is loved,
and he knows it.

But, in the morning when he awakes,
he forgets all that he had done.

He gets out of bed, and washes,
and eats his breakfast of eggs and tea,
and begins his day
believing his day is real.

77

Grandmother Seeta's
Words of Wisdom

The village of Kerilla was terribly divided.

Half the people believed one thing,
the other half another.
Half felt things should be done their way,
the other half opposed them.

People could never agree on anything,
and they hated each other for it.

And all the while,
Grandmother Seeta sat quietly
and knitted.

So bad was life in Kerilla
that families became divided.
Neighbors did not talk to neighbors,
and fighting, hatred, and vile words,
became a way of life.

And all the while,
Grandmother Seeta sat quietly
and knitted.

ഇ൪ൟ

One day, a very important matter
needed to be resolved,
so all the people in the village
gathered in the Great Hall
to decide what must be done.

It did not take long before everyone
began screaming at one another.

Hatred and anger filled the hall,
and nothing was getting done.
Fights broke out, names were called,
and the meeting turned to chaos.

Then a man stood up
and turned to Grandmother Seeta.

"Grandmother, you've not spoken.
What say you
about the issue now at hand?"

Then all became silent and listened intently,
and wondered whose side the old woman
would take.

Grandmother Seeta looked up
from her knitting
and said, with stern authority,

"When you wash your face,
always remember to wash behind your ears!"

She then went back to her knitting.

All was silent.

You could hear the crickets
outside the hall.

It was a giggle that broke the silence,
and then another, and a few more after that,
and soon the hall filled with uproarious laugher
not heard before in Kerilla.

One villager began to talk with another,
then a few more talked as well.
Soon all were talking politely,
even one side to the other.

And the issue that once divided them,
divided them no more.

Life got better in the village of Kerilla.
Finally, things were getting done.
And whenever an issue divided them,
a villager would say,

"Remember Grandmother Seeta's
words of wisdom."

And all would laugh, then talk politely,
and the issue got resolved.

78

Holiest of Holies

There were none more holy, or devout,
then this simple, saintly man.

He lived in total sanctity and virtue,
and was thought by all who knew him
to be among the holiest of the holies.

He studied the Sacred Texts
diligently every day,
and could recite them word for word,
and in the Holy Temple,
would speak before the multitude
on their finer points and meaning.

He devoted his life to helping
the needy and the poor and
he'd spend his days tending to
the sick and to the dying
and throughout the night,

this saintly man
would kneel in prayer and
religious contemplation.

So, it was no surprise
when he left this life,
he went to live in Heaven
to spend eternity among the saints,
the angels and the good.

And, it was no surprise
that his was the closest seat to God.

෨෬

But, when he arrived in Heaven,
he was shocked.

No one was there.

෨෬

He walked the streets of gold,
and searched the marble temples,
and could not find a single soul,
not even God, in Heaven.

He sat alone and waited,
as eons came and went,
yet no soul ever appeared to him,
not even God, in Heaven.

෨෬

One day,
God came running by.

The saintly man cried out,
"Oh, my God, where have you been,
and where are the other souls?"

"Oh, I sent them back to Earth again,"
God replied.

"They needed to lighten up.
I'm on my way to join them.
They're going to need my help."

Then, off he darted.

79

Entering the Hall
of Eternal Bliss

Three souls approached the most glorious
Hall of Eternal Bliss;
a caregiver, a poor woman,
and a woman of wealth.

Standing luminous and powerful
before the entrance,
the mighty Keeper of the
Hall of Eternal Bliss.

ॐ

"Please, 'O Great One,"
beseeched the caregiver, humbly,
her head bowed low to the ground.
"Allow me entrance
into the Hall of Eternal Bliss."

The Keeper, stern and silent,
did not look at her.

"I dedicated my life to helping those
less fortunate,
and sacrificed all in the service of others."
pleaded the caregiver.

"Have I not earned the right to enter?"

The Keeper, stern and silent,
did not look at her.

ॐ

"Please, 'O Great One,"
begged the poor woman, meekly,
her head bowed low to the ground.
"I beg thee, allow me entrance
into the Hall of Eternal Bliss."

The Keeper, stern and silent,
did not look at her.

"I have suffered greatly,
and have gone without my entire life,"
whimpered the poor woman, sobbing piteously.

"Have I not earned the right to enter?"

The Keeper, stern and silent,
did not look at her.

ॐ

The woman of wealth, saying not a word,
walked confidently into the
Hall of Eternal Bliss.

The Keeper bowed and smiled pleasantly
as she passed.

☙❧

The caregiver, and the poor woman,
protested angrily.

"O' mighty Keeper,
why have you allowed this woman
of wealth to pass, are we not more worthy?

Have we not, with our sacrifice and merit,
more right then she to pass?"

The Keeper looked at the two women
and spoke,

"I'm not here to prevent anyone from entering
the Hall of Eternal Bliss.

All may pass through this blessed gate.
Sacrifice and good merit are
not required here."

The caregiver, and the poor woman,
dejected,
walked away and never returned.

They did not want to believe the Keeper.
They felt they were much too entitled.

80

The Gathering

Each year they gather at the ocean's edge
for the rising of a star;
these crones and hermits
of days long forgotten.

Silently they cross the cooling sand,
each carrying an ancient stone,
a crystal of their keeping.

In the still of night, beneath the glow of stars,
they work their many magics;
some alone, some with others,
all in a sacred unison.

There was a time
when these Ancient Ones,
these Grandmothers and Grandfathers,
walked the earth among us
and plied their ancient magic.

But, sadly, our world no longer holds
a place for wise ones such as these.

Yet, they live beyond our seeing
at the boundary of our dreams.

Each year they'll gather,
unbeknownst to us,
to await the rising star,
to gift the world their blessings,
and to craft the world anew.

In the still of the night,
beneath the glow of stars,
these crones and hermits will face the east
to witness a rising blue star.

They'll raise their crystals
above their heads,
and a ray of light
from the Sun that follows,
will pierce each awaiting stone.

A beam of light will then ascend
from each and every stone,
and converge at a single point
high above their heads.

Then bursting forth from this apex point,
multitudes of seeds of light;
new hopes, new dreams, new visions
for a sleeping world below.

Yes, my friends,
each year they gather at the ocean's edge
for the rising of a star;
these crones and hermits
of days long forgotten.

Silently they'll come, and silently they'll go,
and silently in sacred unison,
they'll gift the world their blessings.

81

Tandori Had Two Teachers

Teacher One:

A great scholar,
learned in the arts and sciences.

He taught Tandori the names of stars,
and the proper recitation of the
sacred scriptures.
Tandori learned of heroes of the ancient past,
and the secrets of advanced calculation.

He learned to sing in tune
and to paint with the proper colors.
He learned the languages of other lands
and to speak as if he lived there.

Teacher One
was a great scholar,
learned in the arts and sciences.

Teacher Two:

A simple man,
learned only in love and laughter.

He taught Tandori to see wondrous things
in the shaping of the stars,
and how to fish, skip stones on a pond,
and dance wildly in a meadow.

Oh, and of course,
to sing wonderfully out of tune.

He learned to draw pictures in the sand
and to chuckle as a breeze
blew his drawings away.
He learned the language of the trees,
and the wind,
and the many beasts of the earth.

But, most of all,
he taught Tandori how to laugh.

Teacher Two
was a simple man,
learned in love and laughter

ॐॐ

When Tandori grew to manhood,
he forgot the heroes of the ancient past,
and seldom journeyed to other lands.
He never used advanced calculation,
and rarely read the sacred scriptures.

Tandori only remembered the names
of a star or two.
And he never painted anymore,
and hardly ever sang in tune.

But he taught his son to fish
and dance wildly in a meadow,
and both became masters
at skipping stones on a pond,
and drawing pictures in the sand.

And oh, how they chuckled
as a breeze blew their drawings away.

They would often speak to the wind,
and the trees,
and the wild beasts of the earth
and they'd lay for hours beneath
the night sky,
their minds dancing in wild imagination.

And, of course, they sang
wildly out of tune,
much to the dismay of passersby.

ॐ

Tandori forgot many things
taught to him by
Teacher One.

But he never forgot how to laugh.

82

The Child Who Could

The young girl played in the Enchanted
Forest.

She loved to fly high over the treetops,
and play tag with her friends, the birds.
Together with her playmates, the sylphs,
she'd soar along the rivers,
and spin and loop
above the emerald meadows.

She was happy. She was free.

But,
when she told her loving parents
all that she had done,
her loving parents scolded her and said,
"Don't talk of such foolishness!
People cannot do such things!"

She never flew again.

ಎೞ

The young girl played in the Enchanted
Forest.

She loved to talk with the wild things.

Her friends, the squirrels, chattered happily
of secret places filled with nuts,
and the spiders spun heroic tales.

She knew the songs of the forest birds,
and listened intently as the ancient trees
shared their ancient wisdom.

She was happy. She was free.

But,
when she told her loving parents
all that she had done,
her loving parents scolded her and said,
"Don't talk of such foolishness!
People cannot do such things!"

She never talked with wild things again.

ಎೞ

The young girl played in the Enchanted
Forest.

She loved to dance with her friends,
the nature spirits.

She'd dream with the sylphs,
and swim in the forest pools with the undine.
She'd lie on her back in the meadows
to feel the warmth of the sun,
a gift to her from the salamanders
and she'd play 'hide and seek'
with the gnomes.

She was happy. She was free.

But,
when she told her loving parents
all that she had done,
her loving parents scolded her and said,
"Don't talk of such foolishness!
People cannot do such things!"

৪৩

She flew no more with sylphs,
she talked no more with wild things.
she danced no more with nature spirits,
nor entered again
the Enchanted Forest.

In time, she forgot there was such a place,
and all too soon, grew up.

83

Amil and
the Most Beautiful Flower

A Master and his disciples sat on the
edge of a cliff
overlooking a splendid valley.

He was instructing them in the
complex teachings of the Sacred Texts,
and delving deeply
into the nature of existence.

His disciples listened with rapt attention.

Much knowledge had they gained
from this wise teacher,
and thirsty were they for more;
except for one,

Amil,

who was off preparing their meals,
singing gaily to himself.

Amil never joined in such discussions;
too far over his head were they.

He'd sleep through the times of meditation,
and was always bored by the readings
of the Sacred Texts.

He never paid attention to the
grand discussions of universal truths,
for often he was much too preoccupied
in marveling at the complex wonder
of a flower.

Amil was a simple man, with simple ways.

He was happiest when he was of service
to his beloved Master,
and to his beloved brother disciples.

He'd wash their robes and prepare
their food,
and do all the things that needed to be done,
so the others had time to learn.

One day, the Master noticed a most
beautiful flower growing on the side
of the cliff on the far side of the deep
and narrow gorge.

He much desired this most beautiful flower.

His disciples, wanting to please him,
planned, and studied, and discussed
in great detail,
complex strategies for getting over the deep
and dangerous chasm to the cliff
on the other side.

Many hours passed,
and still, they could find no solution.

When Amil heard of his Master's desire,
he put down the cloths he was washing,
went to the edge of the cliff,
walked gaily upon the air,
and picked that most beautiful flower
awaiting there.

Then he returned,
gave the most beautiful flower
to his beloved Master,
and went back to cleaning the cloths.

84

The Woman Who Had Everything

Unlike the people of her village,
she did not have a big home, and many horses,
and a large family of her own.
She did not have acres of land, or gold,
or other precious things.

But she was contented, nonetheless.

She lived in a modest cottage
a mile outside of town,
and farmed a tiny patch of earth
no bigger than her home.

She planted flowers and healing herbs
in a garden by a stream,
and her only family where the birds
and squirrels who lived within her tree.

But she was contented, nonetheless.

She did not have a horse to work
her tiny patch of earth,
but the land grew abundantly anyway
with all manner of wonderful things,
and if she needed to be somewhere,
she'd be there right on time.

And, although she had no gold or silver,
strangely, whatever she needed or wanted,
she'd have in plentiful supply.

One day, two travelers, walking by her
modest cottage,
stopped and asked for water.

She gave them some
and graciously asked if they would stay
and have a bite to eat.

The two travelers accepted her kind offer,
gratefully, and they all sat at an empty table
beneath her spreading tree.

The woman then closed her eyes.

Suddenly, there appeared before them
a most amazing feast.
The two travelers gasped in amazement
at what they just had seen.

When they finished the meal,
she closed her eyes again,

and everything just vanished,
and the table was empty once again.

The two travelers gasped again in amazement
at what they just had seen.

The meal finished, the two travelers
thanked the woman for her kindness,
and continued on their way,
much bewildered by all that they had seen.

Even to this day, they talk of this
amazing woman, and what they'd seen,
and of the most excellent meal
they ever had.

ॐ

The woman, satiated,
sat beneath her spreading tree
among her birds and squirrels,
content.

85

The Demon Within

He heard the terrifying wail of a demon.

So terrifying was the demon's mournful cry,
he built a wall around himself
to keep the monster out.

He built his wall of the hardest stone,
and high enough that nothing
could climb over,
and since he made no doors or gates,
nothing could come in.

He felt safe, if only for a little while.

ଞ୍ଚଓଷ

However, as time would have it, he heard the
demon's mournful scream again,
this time coming from within the walls
he built solidly around him.

You see, beloved,
when you think you wall a demon out,
in truth, you wall it in.

He was now in great terror.

The walls were too high to climb,
and there were no doors to exit.
The fort he built to keep him safe
now became his prison.

How can he escape?
What was he to do?

Remember this, beloved,
'No matter how impossible things
may seem,
there's always a way out.'

ಶಾಓ

He noticed, for the first time, a door
beneath his feet, his only exit.

But, as he went to open it, he heard the
demon's fearsome cry coming from the
other side, deep beneath the ground.

What was he to do?

Should he stay and wait for his demise,
or face the beast within?

He chose to face the demon.

ॐ

With much fear and trepidation,
he opened the door
and descended a narrow stairway
into the darkness far below.

The deeper he went, the louder
the demon's cry,
the further he went,
the more vile the demon's scent.

He was getting closer now
to the lair of the raging beast.

ॐ

When he reached the bottom of the stairs,
he found himself in a dark chamber
lit only by a single candle.

The place was cold and damp,
and had the vile scent
of lost hope and putrefying dreams.

All was still and silent,
except for the sound of breathing
somewhere in the darkness.

Suddenly, he saw a shadow move
at the far end of the room,
then two red eyes glowing
in the dim of candlelight.

The demon crept slowly from the shadows,
its hateful gaze steady upon him.

So hideous and foul a creature
no man had ever seen,
and the hatred in its burning eyes
was deep and unrelenting.

Its nails, long and sharp,
could tear a man in two,
and it had but one thing on its mind,
and one thing in its heart,
to kill the man before him.

Never once, in this poor man's life,
had he ever felt such terror,
for he knew he soon would die
a most hideous, gruesome death.

Remember this, beloved,
'No matter how impossible things
may seem,
there's always a way out.'

Then, somewhere deep inside the man,
a primal voice sprang out,

"Stop, demon, stop!
I command you not to harm me!"

The creature, startled and confused,
stopped several feet away,
and at that moment, he recognized
the demon there before him.

"It is you!" the man cried out.

"I know you now!
I birthed you long ago!
You're the child of my shame,
the offspring of my rage.

Denying you, I locked you up
in this dark and hidden place."

སོ་ལོ

His terror left and was replaced
by a profound pain and sadness,
and in his heart was deep remorse
for all in life he'd hidden,
and for this sad and lonely beast
that hung its head before him.

"I created you, my child,
and locked you in this lonely place.
I then denied you were a part of me,
and for that, I'm truly sorry.

But you shall terrify no more,
nor shall you ever harm me.

I command you now, my darker self,
show me where to exit,

for you and only you, my child,
can point me to my freedom.”

The hideous creature, so lonely and in
such pain, a single tear
rolling down its cheek,
took its long and sharpened claw
and sliced an opening in the wall.

On the other side, a magnificent garden,
and waiting there were God and Goddess,
and his beloved Higher Self.

But before the man passed through,
he turned to his sad and lonely demon,
and said,

“Although you cannot come with me,
I promise I'll not forget you.
And whenever you call to me again,
I promise I will come
and tend to your hurt and sorrow.

I'll give you love, and heal your pain,
and in time, when you are ready,
you'll come and join me here
not as a demon,
but as a healed and valued part of me.

He entered the garden
to the awaiting arms of God and Goddess,
and his beloved Higher Self,
and into the eternal embrace of
All That Is.

ജ‍ൻ

The demon stayed behind,
for there was hatred still inside him,
though much less than before.

ജ‍ൻ

As the man attends to his pain and hurt,
and nurtures it with love
and understanding,
the anger will lessen more and more,
and his demon, too, will exit.

Remember, beloved,
'No matter how impossible things
may seem, or terrifying,
there's always a way out,
no matter how thick your walls.'

86

The Artist and the Fisherman

A young man sat on the bank of an
endless sea.

Gazing out upon the water,
he saw not the beauty of the waves,
nor the multi-colored sky at the
setting of the sun,
for his heart was burdened
by the difficult times
his life was passing through.

ℴℴ

Then along came an Artist and a Fisherman.

They sat beside him on the bank of the
endless sea
and marveled at the beauty and the majesty
of the rolling waves and crimson sky.

Noticing the young man's absent gaze,

the Artist asked,
"What troubles you, my son?"

To which the young man replied,
"I feel so dark and empty.

Why is life so difficult at times,
and filled with so much shadow?
Why can't life be easier
and always bright and sunny?"

The Artist replied,

"Sometimes, in life, you're happy,
sometimes, in life, you're sad.
Sometimes you have the good,
sometimes, you have the bad;
this is the way our life must be
to give it depth and meaning.

Think of life as a painted canvas.
Take away the shadows
and life will have but two dimensions.

Darkness and shadows
make life more real.
Their purpose is to help us grow
to discover more the light."

The Fisherman added,

"Though fishes live within the sea,
they know nothing of the water,
it's only when you pull them out,
do they know what water is.

Love is the sea in which we swim,
yet we know nothing of its water,
it's only when we're pulled from it,
do we learn what true love is.

And like the fish who learns of water
when he's pulled away from it,
you know of love in those darkened times
when you're pulled away and lose it.

The young man smiled
and thanked the Artist and the Fisherman,
for now, he understood.

The three sat on the bank of an endless sea,
and marveled at the beauty of the waves,
and the multi-colored sky
at the setting of the sun.

A storm will come in a day or two,
but that's okay;
storms make good days all the brighter.

87

The Compassionate Thing to Do

The woman was hungry, so they gave
her food.

They felt good about themselves.
It was the compassionate thing to do.

ഩരു

The woman had no place to live,
so they built her a splendid house.

They felt good about themselves.
It was the compassionate thing to do.

ഩരു

The woman was poor, so they
gave her money.

They felt good about themselves.
It was the compassionate thing to do.

The woman's children could not
read or write,
so they sent them to the finest school
where they graduated at the top
of their class,
although they still could not read,
or write.

They felt good about themselves.
It was the compassionate thing to do.

When the woman became ill, they got her
the finest care.

They felt good about themselves.
It was the compassionate thing to do.

Because the woman lacked what others
had,
they gave her what others had,
and more.

They felt good about themselves.
It was the compassionate thing to do.

When she got old, and her fingers
became sore and gnarly,
they cut them off.

They felt good about themselves.
It was the compassionate thing to do.

෮෮෮

When it became difficult for her to walk,
they cut off both her legs.

They felt good about themselves.
It was the compassionate thing to do.

෮෮෮

When the woman became old and infirm,
they killed her.

They felt good about themselves.
It was the compassionate thing to do.

88

Knowing

They gathered in the Great Hall
and listened in rapt attention
as one by one, the greatest minds
lectured one and all.

When they finished talking,
and it was time to answer questions,
a young girl in the audience stood
and politely asked her question.

"Where can I find, *knowing?*"

The Scientist answered,

"Well, first there's up, and then there's down,
depending on the laws involved,
and it all begins with a hypothesis,
and slowly builds from there.

You take the biggest thing you find
and try to make it smaller,
then find the smallest thing you can
and try to make it bigger.

In short:
$E = MC^2$

⁔⁔⁔

The Mathematician answered,

"You square the number, then multiply,
then calculate the hypotenuse,
then add the sum of your equation
to find the sum of x.

Place your numerator on the denominator,
making sure it does not fall down,
then divide infinity by the whole,
making sure you show your work.

In short:
$MC^2 = E$

⁔⁔⁔

The Poet answered,

"Listen to the singing stars dancing
in the magenta sky
and hear the eternal laughter
of the dappled leaves on high.

'Tit woo! Tit woo!'
sings the goonie bird

'Tit woo
to
you
too'
says
I

In short:
It's all in the rhyme and the rhythm,
and in the way it looks on the paper."

꽃❀

The Philosopher answered,

"*Knowing* is but an ephemeral thing,
depending on the knower.
It shifts and changes over time,
but then, time's an illusion,
so it really doesn't matter.

'Knowing,' like the knower, is unknowable,
an object of subjective reasoning,
and I'm not really speaking to you,
because I'm not really here.

In short:
Life is a giant lunch bag,
and we, a mere ham sandwich."

꽃❀

The Artist answered,

"Reach into your soul, my dear,
it's there you'll find your answer.

Splash bright colors on the 'knowing,'
and stay away from form.
Spurn all convention! Let it fly!
Follow the rules no more,
except for the rules I give you;
they're okay.

In short:
Stay away from pastels, my dear,
they're oh, so not in style!"

ೞೲ

The Teacher answered,

"Pay attention in my class,
and listen to me well,
and if you do your homework,
and pass all tests and quizzes,
then you'll surely know.

'Knowing' is the gift I give
to those who meet my standards.

In short:
A – you know exceptionally well
B – you know well enough, indeed
C – you're average in your knowing
D – you know enough to pass
F – you dummy! You know nothing!"

ॐॐ

The Theologian answered,

"*Knowing* cannot be known, my child,
God's too big for that,
better to leave such weighty matters
to the Temple Priests.

But, what I surely know is this,
if you attend the Holy Temple once a week,
especially on the High Days,
and if you tithe ten percent
of all your earnings,
you'll surely go to Heaven.

And, while we're on the subject,
give to science what belongs to science,
but the rest belongs to us, goddammit!"

The Scientist, and the Mathematician,
nodded politely in agreement.

"In short:
What we do know is this,
three angels can fit on the head of a pin,
two skinnies, and a fat one."

ॐॐ

When the young girl left the Great Hall,
she was dazed and much confused,
more so than before.

"Where can I find *knowing?*"

She asked herself many times,
but could not find the answer.

ෂ෬

One day, as she watched her little
brother gaze in awe
at a snowflake on a mushroom,
she knew.

ෂ෬

There's knowing in the wonder,
and wonder in the knowing.

89

Some Things
Are Just Worth Saving

In our lives, we pick and choose
what we give meaning to,
some are good, some are bad,
others in between.

And since our lives are but reflections
of what we give meaning to,
the pains and hurts,
the hopes and joys,
from all the meanings stored inside,
are but reflections, too.

Children in the schoolyard bullied him,
and called him vile names.

For some strange and hidden reason,
this was valuable to him.

So, he took what the children said to him
and tied each neatly in a little bow,
and stored them deep inside
to be addressed another day.

But, I guess some things are just
worth saving.

දාය

His father once said to him,
"You'll never amount to much, my boy.
It's best, you learn this now."

For some strange and hidden reason,
this was valuable to him.

So, he took what his father said to him
and tied it neatly in a little bow,
and stored it deep inside
to be addressed another day.

But, I guess some things are just
worth saving.

දාය

His teacher said to him, on the day of
his graduation,
"You're really not that bright, my boy,
and that's a simple fact.

Make the most with the little you've got,
and I wish you all the best."

For some strange and hidden reason,
this was valuable to him.

So, he took what his teacher said to him
and tied it neatly in a little bow,
and stored it deep inside
to be addressed another day.

But, I guess some things are just
worth saving.

⊰⊱

He fell in love and sincerely thought
their love would be forever.

But, without warning, and in a
fit of rage, she pierced his heart by saying,

"I've never truly loved you, John.
You're really not worth loving.
So this is it, and this is that.
Consider our love now over!"

For some strange and hidden reason,
this was valuable to him.

So, he took what his lover said to him
and tied it neatly in a little bow,
and stored it deep inside
to be addressed another day.

But, I guess some things are just
worth saving.

ಌಌ

His mother said to him many times,
"Don't have sex before marriage, John,"
and "Always eat your squash."

He threw those away.

ಌಌ

We pick and choose what we keep and save;
their value's in the keeping.
Some things make us light and free,
others much imprisoned.

But know this and know it well.

*"All we store of hurt and pain
must someday be addressed."*

Our growth demands it

ಌಌ

We're never bound by the words and
deeds of others
unless they're just worth saving.

90

The Ministers of Kushtan

A great flood ravished the
land of Kushtan.
Many were killed,
including all of Kushtan's Ministers.

Since the people were sorely in
need of governance,
a committee was selected
to find ministers to replace them.

The committee immediately sought
the counsel of a great and holy sage
who lived in the remote mountains
to the south.

Kneeling before the holy man,
they implored him.

"O' wise Sage,
we come to seek your guidance

in finding those who will best govern
our poor and ravished land.

We seek a
Minister of Education.

What is your sage advice?"

The holy man answered.

"Go among the people,
find the brightest one you can.

This one must possess the gift
of clarity and patience."

౭౦౧౩

"We seek a
Minister of Science.

What is your sage advice?"

The holy man answered,

"Go among the people,
find one with the most curious mind.

This one must have the gift of separating
reality from illusion."

౭౦౧౩

"We seek a
Minister of Defense.

What is your sage advice?"

The holy man answered,

"Go among the people,
find a champion of the weak.

This one must possess the gift
of strength and kindness both."

෫෧ඏ

"We seek a
Minister of Art and Culture.

What is your sage advice?"

The holy man answered,

"Go among the people,
find the most awakened heart.

This one must possess that special gift
of balancing light and dark."

෫෧ඏ

"We seek a
Minister of Justice.

What is your sage advice?"

The holy man answered,

"Go among the people,
find the most honest one you can.

This one must possess the gift
of knowing truth from lies."

"Finally, great Sage, we seek a
Minister of Government;
one who knows the workings
of politics and state.

What is your sage advice?"

The holy man answered,

"Go among the people,
find the least intelligent among them.

No special gifts required."

91

A Gift of Laughter

The people of the village did not just love
the old man; they adored him.

Wherever he went, and to whomever he met,
he would lighten their hearts with kindness
and ignite their spirits with laughter.

To this day,
the people talk of him with deep affection;
but most of all, they laugh.

Whenever someone in the village died,
leaving loved ones deep in pain,
the old man sat and held them tight
as they cried away their grief.

In time, he'd have them smiling
from the stories that he told;
beloved stories of their dear departed

with those precious cherished memories
those treasured stories hold.

Eventually, they'd laugh.

ॐ

Wherever hearts were broken,
and heavy with hurt or fear,
the old man came, and spirits brightened,
people would laugh,
and everything would be better in the end.

ॐ

Children wanted to be with him always.
He shared their wonder and their joy.
And when they laughed freely,
and danced in the sun,
the old man joined in too.

Grown-up now,
they share with their children his
magical stories,
along with loving memories of the kind old man
who made them laugh,
and their children would laugh, too.

ॐ

So, when the old man died, all in the village
felt the loss.

No one could speak through the tears
that flowed, and a pall descended over
everyone and everything.

For all that was bright and wonderful,
and all that was joyous and light,
left them now, forever.

They buried him beneath his favorite tree,
and placed flowers on his grave
and all in the village gathered around
and stood in silence, or wept,
from pain so difficult to bear.

Suddenly,
along came a squirrel lopping merrily about.

He sniffed and scurried,
and scurried and sniffed,
then crouched upon the old man's grave
and peed.

All were shocked and speechless,
by such an act of disrespect.

But, one small child began to giggle.
Then another. Then another.
Then a couple more,
till everyone burst out in uproarious laughter.

So loud and free was the joyful sound,
it could be heard for miles away.

ಬಿಂ

No one could see the old man
leaning against his favorite tree,
laughing hysterically at everyone
enjoying his parting gift.

Epilogue

And, on the ninety-first night, after
the last story was told,
the Great and Holy Sinjin-Ka closed his eyes
and returned once more to Eternal Bliss,
and into the nurturing womb of the Divine.

And the body that once was Sinjin-Ka,
slowly turned to mist.

And all that remained of this wise and holy man
were ninety-one scented flowers
blooming brightly where once he sat.

In the distant valley far below,
people, to this very day,
smell the blessed fragrance
of the

Scented Flowers of Sinjin-Ka.

About the Author

Martin Hart is author of the books, *The C.O.R.E. Principles* (ASAT Press), *The Magic of the Scented Flowers* (ASAT Press) and co-author, along with Skye Alexander of *The Best Meditations on the Planet: 100 techniques to Beat Stress, Improve Health, and Create Happiness in Just Minutes a Day* (Fair Winds Press).

Martin is the founder and president of the American Society of Alternative Therapists (ASAT™) and has been in private counseling and alternative health education for more than forty years. Since 1978, Martin has conducted workshops and lectures throughout the United States and internationally on alternative healing and other life-enhancing subjects. He has taught at some of the largest corporations in Asia, as well as top colleges and research facilities. In the late 1980s, Martin combined a series of highly effective healing modalities with his unique counseling approach producing the innovative and remarkably successful healing system *ASAT*™ *C.O.R.E. Counseling.*

As a result of the efficacy of this approach, Martin started training ASAT™ C.O.R.E. Counselors in 1990 to meet the growing number of people seeking this road to greater self-awareness and healing.

Martin still travels the United States and internationally conducting his trainings as well as related lectures and workshops. His courses and seminars have been featured in the Wall Street Journal, The Boston Globe, The London Sunday Telegraph, and other publications. He has also appeared on popular national and international talk radio programs discussing his unique work.

To contact him, and to get more information regarding his trainings and workshops, visit ASAT's website at www.asat.org.

Other Books by Martin Hart

* ***The Magic of the Scented Flowers:*** *Unfolding the healing power of The Scented Flowers of Sinjin-Ka in crafting an elegant and magical life.* (ASAT Press)

* ***The C.O.R.E. Principles:*** *ASAT™ C.O.R.E. Counseling and the Pursuit of Becoming More.* (ASAT Press)

* ***The Best Meditations on the Planet:*** *100 techniques to Beat Stress, Improve Health, and Create Happiness in Just Minutes a Day.* By Martin Hart and Skye Alexander (Fair Winds Press)

Books can be purchased in paperback or ebook formats online or in local bookstores. Signed copies can be purchased through ASAT Press (www.asat.org)